BETTY

Fire in the Wind

A Beech Tree Paperback Book
NEW YORK

The Library of Congress has cataloged the Greenwillow Books
edition of *Fire in the Wind* as follows:
Levin, Betty.
Fire in the wind / by Betty Levin.
p. cm.
Summary: In 1947 in Maine, a raging fire that threatens their farm
and the nearby town makes the members of Meg's extended family
see their strained relationships in a new light. ISBN 0-688-14299-0
[1. Family life—Maine—Fiction. 2. Brothers and sisters—Fiction. 3.
Cousins—Fiction. 4. Fires—Fiction. 5. Maine—Fiction.] I. Title.
PZ7.L5759Fi 1995 [Fic]—dc20 94-48801 CIP AC

10 9 8 7 6 5 4 3 2 1
First Beech Tree Edition, 1997
ISBN 0-688-15495-6

For Claudia and Lennie
and for Martha

PROLOGUE

Meeting House Road begins at Charity Corners and ends where it runs into Alder Swamp Road. Few people go that way unless they are heading for Charity Pond.

On this still, hot October morning Gus Browning brakes as the road enters the darkness of the woods. Although he cannot see very far ahead, he is no stranger to this place. He has hunted here in years gone by, has cut and hauled timber. But now he is old and slow. So is his truck. It has been repaired so often that none of it resembles the original vehicle. Since his horse has gone permanently lame, Gus has even used parts from his old cart to shore up the wooden truck bed, which is used to haul feed to pigs and pigs to market. The solid tailgate that can drop down to become a loading ramp is held upright by two chains.

One of those chains has been shaken loose and drags behind. As the truck jounces along, the chain strikes stone after stone until it gets so hot you wouldn't want to touch it. The sparks it sets off cool and die in seconds. But one stone is struck so sharply that the chain flies up, spraying sparks to the roadside.

Most of the sparks cool before they fall. But two of them, like seeds tossed in the wind, seek nourishment where they lie. This bed is especially fertile for tiny new seeds of fire. One of them nestles in the fist of a brown leaf. The other rolls from the stem of a dead evergreen branch, filtering down among fir needles that are so light and lacy they let in plenty of air.

Air and fuel, essentials to the life of a fire.

Yet there is a pause, a waiting instant while the needles smoke and curl. Then they blaze.

1

In this first spurt of life the spark that has taken root shoots up and flowers, scattering new seeds that send forth more seedlings. Then it seems to rest, perhaps to gather strength.

The next car to turn onto the road isn't nearly as old as Gus Browning's truck, and it has a new paint job to spruce it up. Its backseat is loaded with mail already sorted for a rural route. The mail carrier, Mike Yeadon, has come this way to check on the lodge, the only grand summer place on Charity Pond. He detours here a couple of times a week, always keeping an eye out for Miss Trilling's cat, which disappeared the day before she left for the winter.

Mike notices a smudge of smoke just off to the side. He jams on the brakes. After jumping out of the car, he kicks the smoking debris onto the road, where he can stamp out the fire. But he is not aware of the curled leaf that shelters the other spark. He doesn't realize that he has kicked it free as well.

Continuing on, he guesses that someone careless with a cigarette, probably someone from out of state, must have gone by moments before him. Everyone in Maine knows by now how tinder dry the woods are. He thinks it was a lucky break coming right behind the careless smoker.

Meanwhile, the second spark nibbles through the center of the leaf. Released, it bursts into flame and spreads hungrily outward. First it consumes what remains of the sheltering leaf. Next, expanding with energy, it seizes on needles still warm from the first flame. Feeding rapidly, it seeks other leaves and then the stunted stems of roadside asters and pearly everlasting.

Still famished, it devours all it can reach. Here are twigs and woody brush, brittle and thirsting for rain. There stands a patch of cranberry, a few shriveled fruits still attached. The wiry cranberry seethes and twists before exploding into a blaze that wings through sedge and grass toward the dried-up swamp. The flame slams into the base of a birch tree whose bark, already shredded by porcupine and rabbits, spreads its papery fingers to receive the fire.

It is only a matter of seconds now until flames are climbing the trunk, red and yellow vines aflower, embracing this first tree, but not the only one it will consume.

Alder Swamp Road forks as it emerges from the woods. One branch loops around Charity Pond, and another joins the road that parallels the railroad tracks and climbs toward the next town. Not far from this road and the railroad line and the river, firefighters dig a trench to keep an older, trouble-some fire from spreading onto parched farmland that leads to the center of town.

One fighter is a boy, big for his age and not very quick. But he sticks to the task, digging where he must and pausing from time to time to turn and whack out live embers with his shovel. Sweat pours into his eyes, which already sting from the smoke-filled air.

Once when he pauses to slap out a tiny flame that has erupted from the ground like some fast-growing weed, he cannot bring his shovel down to smash it. It seems to him a wild creature, newly born, poised between life and death. He is a giant bearing a weapon raised for slaughter. He watches the tiny tongue dart this way and that, lapping at orange flowers until they open and stretch and beckon nearby twigs and grasses. Nothing can resist the lure of this beautiful, deadly creature that has sprung living from the earth.

Laying aside his shovel, the boy crouches, his hands cir-cling as if to shelter the fiery nestling, to keep it from harm.

"Hey, Orin, wake up!" someone shouts at him. And a boot stamps out the flame, extinguishing the marvelous, writhing thing whose birth he witnessed seconds before and whose death he must witness now as well.

IMeg Yeadon heard the younger kids run out for recess. Half her mind was on the division problems Mrs. Boudreau was writing on the blackboard. The other half was on her brother, Paul, who had just started first grade this year and wasn't too good at defending himself against the bigger kids in the schoolyard.

Meg was pretty sure she could hear his voice raised against the others. Listening hard, she was able to single out Joan Barter's mean-sounding taunt. Joan was the bully of the lower grades.

Meg stabbed her pencil into her workbook. As soon as the point snapped, she headed for the pencil sharpener, which was beside the window that overlooked the schoolyard. Cranking the sharpener handle as slowly as she could, she peered outside. It looked as though all eleven kids from the lower grades were in on a game, tossing an odd-shaped ball over Paul's head. Only it wasn't a ball. Meg knew that. It was a huge, perfectly formed paper wasp nest. It floated from hand to hand, while Paul darted first at one kid and then at another in an effort to retrieve his treasure.

Meg glanced around the classroom. Mrs. Boudreau was still at the blackboard. Meg figured it would only a take a minute or two to straighten out the situation in the schoolyard. She could be back at her desk before Mrs. Boudreau noticed she was gone.

Meg slipped out through the open door. Miss Wylie, the lower-grades teacher, who should have been paying attention to the kids in the yard, was nowhere to be seen.

Meg took the steps two at a time and tore around the side of the school. Pelting across the yard, she forgot to be careful

4

about keeping quiet. "That's Paul's," she bellowed as she charged into the knot of kids.

"That's Paul's," someone mimicked. It had to be Joan, who had dared to defy Meg last year when her cousin Orin had been the butt of Joan's teasing.

"He said it was his cousin's," another kid retorted.

"It is," Meg responded. "Was. Orin found it in the woods. It still had wasps. He got stung."

"Poor Orin," cried Joan. "Poor borin' Orin."

Joan, who was in the third grade, was already bigger than Meg. She had a voice to match her size and used it to belt out Judy Garland songs and to make fun of kids she didn't like. Just now that voice mocking Orin hit Meg like a punch in the stomach. Hot all over, she sucked in hard. Even last year it hadn't been easy to tackle Joan. But Meg had had years of practice with bigger kids, who never regarded scrawny Meg Yeadon as a threat. This time she caught Joan sideways, with one leg bent and twisted just enough to trip her up. Down went the bully, still clutching the delicate paper wasp nest.

Paul wailed, "No!"

The other kids backed off as Miss Wylie appeared. "Meg Yeadon," she snapped, "get off. Joan Barter, get up."

"She took my brother's wasp nest," Meg protested. "She was throwing it."

"Look what you've done," Miss Wylie scolded as the nest rolled away from Joan, gray shreds dragging in the dirt.

Meg glared at Joan. "You broke it," she said.

"It can be wrapped up again," Joan answered. "Only one side's busted."

"It was perfect," Meg charged. "Now it's spoiled." She glanced at Paul, who had picked up the crumpled nest and was trying to pat it back into shape. "Let me try," Meg said to him.

"No," said Paul. "You knocked her on top of it."

Meg was sent back to her classroom. She could feel the other kids' attention, even though they all had their backs to her as she walked inside. It was the most interesting thing that had happened in school since this morning, when they had heard the fire whistle blow and trucks and cars had headed down Meeting House Road.

Mrs. Boudreau acted as though nothing were amiss. She let Meg get all the way to her desk and partway into her chair before saying, "Meg, won't you need your pencil to finish your work?"

Meg had to get up and walk back to the pencil sharpener. She allowed herself one glimpse into the schoolyard. There was Paul, sitting on the dusty ground, trying to blow air into the wasp nest as if it were a balloon he could inflate with his breath.

2 Joyce Leblanc stopped before turning up her driveway.

"Want to come in?" she asked Meg.

Meg did want to, but she knew she would be in even worse trouble if Paul went on home without her. So she said she guessed not.

"What did Mrs. Boudreau write to your folks?" asked Joyce.

"I don't know," Meg told her. "The envelope's sealed."

"Well, what did she say to you?"

"The usual. That I should tend to my own business. That she'd thought I was all finished with fighting since Orin left school."

Joyce turned to Paul and said, "You don't know how lucky you are to have a sister that sticks up for you."

Paul kicked at a stone. He didn't speak.

6

Meg trudged on, followed by Paul. She slowed, hoping he would walk beside her, but he refused to catch up.

Meg had to figure out how to handle Mrs. Boudreau's letter. Since this was Mom's late day at the telephone exchange, either Gran or Dad should read it before Aunt Helen got her hands on it.

Meg pretended to examine the bleached stubble in the fields that had failed to grow a second hay crop. The field on the right side of the road ended at the orchard, where Toby and June stood head to tail under a dusty apple tree. As Meg and Paul approached, the horses raised their heads to look at them. Usually they were at work in the woodlot with Orin. But not today. Orin and Eddie Kresky had gone over to Croyden to help fight the fires that kept cropping up along the railroad tracks.

Not a proper job for a boy, Gran had argued, especially a boy like Orin. But Orin had pointed out that they were letting guys out of high school to help on the firelines. So he was away, and Toby and June were left to browse in the orchard with wasps buzzing around the shriveled apples at their feet.

Glimpsed first through the bare apple trees, the farmhouse looked almost like three unattached houses built right next to one another. But the big house that belonged to Gran and Uncle Frank and Aunt Helen was not separate from the little house where Meg and Paul lived with their parents, nor was the back house apart, even though it stood slightly behind the others. Like Paul keeping his distance from Meg but still connected.

Zac came down to the road to meet them, wagging his tail and ducking his head. Meg stooped to hug him before noticing that he had rolled in something smelly.

"Now you stink," Paul told her. He ran ahead to the swing that hung from the maple in their dooryard.

Meg paused and looked over at Paul, who had carefully set

the bashed wasp nest on the ground. "You coming?" she asked him.

Hiking himself onto the swing, he shook his head.

"Aren't you thirsty?"

He shook his head some more and began to pump. The rope creaked as the swing responded.

All at once Meg saw herself in his place, not at Paul's age but two and a half years ago, just before Champ was shipped overseas. It was the end of his leave. In the midst of the good-byes she had gone clammy cold and had had to get out of the house. So she had run away to the swing. She had pumped and pumped, leaning back and then digging at the sky to gain distance from the ground.

She hadn't realized Champ had come outdoors until he had caught the swing midflight. He had held it suspended for a moment before lowering it and going around to face her.

"You look out for Orin," he had ordered.

"I always do," she had answered without meeting his eyes.

Champ had nodded. "Just like I did. Don't let anyone fool around with him."

"I won't. I'll take care of Orin till you get back."

Champ had shaken his head. "I'm not coming back," he had told her. "Anyways, not to stay."

"What do you mean?" Now she did look at him.

"I've been to real places, Meg. Cities and that. Nothing could keep me here now. So you'll be the oldest."

"No, I won't. Orin's nearly thirteen."

Champ had tapped his head. "Not up here, Meggie. Not where it counts."

Meg had almost kicked Champ away. How could he announce that he was leaving for good when everyone was counting on giving him a hero's welcome when the war was over? "Does Uncle Frank know?" she had asked him.

Steadying the swing, Champ had thrust his face close to

8

hers. "Of course not. And you'd better not let on. I only told you on account of Orin."

Afterward Meg had wondered what Champ would have said if she had told him she was going away, too, as soon as she was old enough. But at the time, while he fixed her with his intense blue eyes, she hadn't uttered a word. Probably if she had spoken, it would have been to plead with him not to desert her.

"No need to trouble the folks at a time like this," Champ had declared. "You promise?"

She had nodded. All her life she had done his bidding just to bask in his approval.

He had grinned at her, his eyes full of laughter. "That's my girl. You've never given me away yet." Stepping back and drawing the swing with him, he had held her aloft for a second before thrusting her away. "So be good," he had told her. "Be bad," he had added with a wink and a jaunty wave.

She had still been swinging when Aunt Helen and Uncle Frank had driven off with him. Two and a half years ago. His voice, his eyes, his ready laugh still all around the place, real as life. But not Champ. Never again Champ.

3 Opening the little house door, which both families used, Meg wondered what her chances were for getting to her room before anyone realized she was home. But the moment she stepped inside, Gran spoke up from the kitchen: "Meg, bring Mrs. Boudreau's note in here." So Mrs. Boudreau had already called and alerted the family. Meg had no choice but to turn into the big kitchen that the Grays and Yeadons shared.

Gran was pouring melted paraffin into jars of clear red jelly.

In spite of what lay ahead, Meg was drawn to the table. She loved to watch the paraffin cloud up as it cooled on the surface.

"Why do you always pour it twice?" she asked, for there was still only a thin waxy film over the new jelly.

Gran explained why the seal held better with two coatings. She must have described the process a dozen times before, but she didn't seem to mind repeating herself, not even this time when she might have suspected that Meg was asking only to put off the scolding that was to come.

But for Meg this was no delaying tactic. Resting her elbows on the table, she stared at the crab apple jelly topped with whitening paraffin. "It's magic," she said to Gran.

"Seems like magic to me, too," Gran replied, "seeing as this is the first season without sugar being rationed. There now." She set the saucepan on the stove. "Let's hear how come you beat up a girl younger than you."

"What did Mrs. Boudreau tell you?" Meg asked as she handed over the letter she had carried home from school. "Anyway," she went on as Gran tore open the envelope and began to read, "Mrs. Boudreau wasn't even there. So how can she know?"

After a moment Gran folded the letter and slipped it into her apron pocket. "I'm asking you, Meg," she said, "not your teacher. If you get a move on, we can have this thing out of the way before anyone else gets mixed up in it."

The veiled threat worked. The trouble with living in a household with more than one family was that all the grownups thought they had a right to act for Meg's parents when they weren't around to deal with her themselves. Uncle Frank and Aunt Helen were nothing like Meg's mother and father, though. They weren't inclined to laugh things off, and they didn't have the patience to talk things out like Gran or Mom and Dad.

Meg said to Gran, "All the kids ganged up against Paul.

10

They had his wasp nest that Orin gave him. He took it to school to show Miss Wylie. Joan was just being mean. Anyway, she's a lot bigger than me, so what difference does it make that she's younger?"

Instead of replying, Gran asked, "What do you suppose would've happened if you'd left it up to Paul and those other children?"

Meg dipped a finger into the paraffin pot. It was almost too hot, but she liked the way the wax clung like a second skin. "I don't know." She waved her hand to cool it off.

"Think ahead to next year. Once they finish the new school addition in town, our Charity Corners school will shut down for good. Paul will be with many more children in his own classroom. How will he learn to get along with them if you keep sticking your nose in his business?"

Meg peeled off the paraffin and rolled it into a ball. She didn't know how to answer Gran. She wasn't even sure now what had made her fly at Joan.

"I gather the wasp nest was smashed," Gran went on. "Don't you imagine Joan and the others would have gotten tired of the game and given the nest back to Paul?"

"I don't know. Maybe."

"You're fire in the wind, Meg, always blowing something up out of nothing."

Meg flared. "It was never nothing, not with Orin."

"Orin isn't your responsibility now. I thought you turned over a new leaf after he left school."

Meg nodded. Last winter, when Orin had stayed out of school after Christmas vacation, Meg had eased into a new and peaceful time there. Until this fall, when Paul started first grade. Then all her worries had surfaced again lest Paul be in for the same kind of misery that had plagued Orin after Champ, his protector, had moved on to the high school.

Gran walked to the stove and lifted off its kerosene tank.

"Will you go down cellar and fill this up? There won't be enough fuel left to get supper cooked."

Meg took the tank from her grandmother, who turned back to reheat the paraffin. Was that all Gran was going to say about the trouble at school? Anyway, what did that mean, fire in the wind? Meg asked her that.

"Maybe I overspoke," Gran told her. "But it does seem to me that you tend to fan the flames most sensible people would put out."

Meg opened the cellar door and descended into the cool dimness below. If only she could come right out and explain that after sticking up for Orin since she was no bigger than Paul, fighting was second nature to her. Why couldn't Gran see that where all Champ ever had to do was threaten kids to make them leave Orin alone, a shrimp of a girl like Meg had to keep proving to them that they couldn't get away with their mean tricks.

She wished she could stay down here, with everything so cool and peaceful. Along with the reek of the kerosene that bubbled into the stove tank, the cellar smelled of apples and carrots and potatoes and turnips. It smelled of the earth itself. Was Gran right about Meg's being fire in the wind? Where were the flames now? Meg couldn't feel them at all.

4 At suppertime Meg could tell that Gran had not yet mentioned the fight. Dad started right in talking about a small fire he'd come across on Alder Swamp Road. He figured it must have just gotten started, because it hadn't really amounted to much. He had scattered the embers and stamped it out in no time.

Uncle Frank said there must have been a second fire then,

soon after, because he and Pete Kresky had gone over there as soon as they heard the fire whistle blow. It had taken quite a few volunteers to put it out.

Aunt Helen shook her head. She supposed those roadside fires were mostly started by someone tossing a cigarette from a car.

Uncle Frank suddenly shoved back his chair. "I'd like to get my hands on the guy," he declared softly. A vein stood out on his forehead. Raising his hands, he played out wringing someone's neck. His face had gone pale, his eyes like black stones. "People like that are no better than murderers; that's how they should be treated." His voice was strangely flat yet full of quiet fury.

Stunned, everyone fell silent.

Finally Gran spoke up. "Maybe you should bring Orin home. Maybe it's too much worry."

"I don't know, Ma." Uncle Frank's voice sounded almost normal now. It was hard for Meg to grasp such a swift mood change. She doubted that even the grown-ups could tell what triggered his rages. "It's not just Orin," he said. "It's the whole situation, people's homes and livestock in danger. Orin's all right. After all, he's been working in the woods close to a year now."

"But that's with Eddie and those that know him," Aunt Helen pointed out. "They understand his limits."

"Listen," Uncle Frank told her, "if he wasn't useful, they'd send him home. Anyhow, some ways he's smarter than he seems."

"Of course he is," Gran agreed. "There's plenty of things Orin can do as well as the next one, especially handling horses. But don't forget, backward or not, he's still a boy."

Meg's father offered to drive over to Croyden tomorrow when he finished his mail route to see how Orin was getting on. But Meg's mother said she could check on him through

13

the telephone exchange. She reminded everyone that the Croyden road was supposed to be kept clear for fire-fighting equipment.

Meg and Paul left the table as soon as they could. Uncle Frank's outbursts were bad enough when they were loud, but somehow this quiet one was scarier.

Paul went outside to call his little black banty hens in for the night. Usually he stood in the dooryard and banged a pie tin with a spoon to get them home. But not tonight, thought Meg. If the racket didn't bother Uncle Frank, the hens surely would.

Paul had raised the two black hens after a raccoon had eaten their mother. The chicks had been so tiny then that they would have been snapped up by the first crow cruising by. So Mom and Dad had let Paul take them inside. "House flowers," Gran had called them. But the first time one messed on the kitchen floor and Aunt Helen declared them a disgrace, they had become Grace and Disgrace as well.

This evening Meg suggested that Paul call them away from the house, keeping the racket out of Uncle Frank's way. But instead of coming to Paul under the maple, the little hens flapped straight to the door. Shouting to them, Paul banged harder. The hens grew frantic. They pecked at the door, squawking and peeping at the same time. Before Meg and Paul could reach them, the door burst open, and Uncle Frank strode out, kicking the hens aside. Screeching, they flew up onto the back house roof, where they raised their cries to new heights.

"Stupid, worthless birds," Uncle Frank muttered as he stumped down the hill to the barn.

"Grace!" wailed Paul. "Disgrace!"

But the little hens refused to leave their perch.

Finally Mom appeared in the doorway and told the children

to come get ready for bed. She promised to cage the hens as soon as they returned.

"They won't," Paul cried. "Uncle Frank kicked them."

"He didn't mean to," Mom answered. "They always come."

"He did so mean to," Meg blurted. "He did it on purpose."

Her mother lowered her voice. "Remember what we've told you, Meg. Your uncle's going through a hard time."

"Why?" asked Paul.

"Because of Champ. Champ was the world to him."

"He still has Orin," Paul said.

"Orin can't be the kind of son Champ was. If Champ hadn't been killed, he would have taken over this farm one day. He was the future."

"Doesn't Uncle Frank like Orin?" Paul asked.

"Don't be silly," Mom replied. "Of course. Frank and Helen love Orin."

Meg hated it when Mom talked like this. Why did she have to shield Uncle Frank and Aunt Helen from the obvious truth? What made Mom think that she could fool Paul, who faced her as she stood in the lighted doorway? Meg, unable to see his face, wondered what he was thinking. But all he said was "If Grace and Disgrace go to sleep up there, they'll be eaten."

Mom heaved a sigh and went back inside. A moment later Dad came out of the back house with a ladder. The children watched him climb to the roof. Then Grace, or Disgrace, let out a wild cry and half tumbled and half flew to the lighted doorway. Dad managed to grab the other hen and stuff her inside his shirt without dropping his flashlight. Both house flowers were safely bedded down in their cage in the back house before Uncle Frank returned from the barn.

Once he was back inside, Meg and Paul kept clear of him, choosing to use the privy out in the back house rather than traipse through the kitchen to get to the new bathroom. They

15

managed to be in bed and looking asleep before Mom came in to remind them to wash.

When Mom stopped beside Meg's bed, Meg guessed that Mom was thinking about waking her. That meant Mom had finally seen Mrs. Boudreau's letter.

Meg drew in a long breath, groaned a little, and rolled onto her stomach. Mom tiptoed out of the room.

5 Waking, Meg thought: rain. Squeezing her eyes tight shut, she listened to the patter against the window. That meant there must be a wind, too. A good storm could put an end to the drought. Everyone would feel better, even Uncle Frank.

The rain sounded fitful, though, with long spells between the pinging that made her think of icicles breaking off the eaves and hitting the side of the house.

Only this wasn't icicle time.

Meg thrust back her sheet and sat up. Opening her eyes, she stared at the window, the panes still filmed with dust. As the next flurry rattled them, she saw that what she had taken for raindrops were nothing more than dead leaves and twigs hurled by the wind.

Voices floated through from the kitchen, louder than usual. Meg couldn't hear Dad. That probably meant he had driven Mom to work before going to the post office. Meg dressed slowly to give Uncle Frank and Aunt Helen time to settle their argument.

She glanced over at Paul. Even though he was six, he still slept like a baby, all curled up and facedown. He needed to get ready for school, but he also needed to stay out of Uncle Frank's way.

16

Meg listened to the argument. Not an argument exactly but a continuation of all the complaints that erupted from time to time like Uncle Frank's temper. They were talking about Orin again, Aunt Helen sounding worried and Uncle Frank sounding fed up. Meg couldn't help feeling that Champ was there between them through everything they said, even though neither of them spoke his name. That seemed to be how they mostly talked to each other, with more left out than included in what they said.

When the radio came on, the voices in the kitchen subsided. The grown-ups were listening to the weather report and a list of new fires spotted from mountain outlooks.

Meg woke Paul and told him to hurry. She ran through the kitchen to the bathroom and brushed her teeth. By the time she was back in the kitchen and sitting down to the plate of bacon and toast that Aunt Helen set before her, someone on the radio was discussing what it would cost the state of Maine if the fire danger interfered with the hunting season. That prompted Uncle Frank to wonder whether yesterday's fire might have been the work of someone up to mischief in the woods off Alder Swamp Road.

"Sometimes people camp down by the pond," Gran said. "After the summer camps are shut up for the winter. They use the outdoor fireplaces. So it could be an accident as well as mischief."

"I guess there's no telling," Frank answered, "unless they're caught at it. Wouldn't I like to be the one to set them straight. They'd never do it again."

Paul, who had come to the table, kept his eyes on his plate.

Aunt Helen said that she had heard that some of the men on the new turnpike construction crew had caught two young guys starting fires for the fun of it. Rumors, said Gran. Still, Uncle Frank responded, prison was too good for guys like that.

Meg glanced at Paul, who was sitting so still he reminded her of a frightened chipmunk trying to look invisible. She supposed that as soon as they were out of the house, she could tell him Uncle Frank didn't really mean all he said. Only she knew she would sound fake, as if she were copying Mom. She knew she would be just about as unconvincing, too.

6 At school everyone was talking about yesterday's fire. No one sounded worried, only excited. After all, Alder Swamp wasn't very far from Charity Corners. Everyone wished the fire had waited until school let out so that they could have gone to watch.

"Over to Croyden," Simon Farris declared, "they're sending in tanks to fight that fire. Army tanks."

Mrs. Boudreau corrected him. "Not really tanks, Simon."

"Yes, they are. My father said so."

Mrs. Boudreau said more firmly, "Those are tank trucks, not tanks. Most of our small fire departments don't have water carriers or pumps. Now let's leave the fires to the firefighters and get to work."

The children squirmed and sighed. They all knew someone, or someone who knew someone, who had gone with shovel and rake to help control fires that had sprung up in neighboring communities.

"To get back on track," Mrs. Boudreau said with a smile, almost as if she had made a joke, "let's talk about what's coming later on this month."

The children faced her in silence.

"Getting back on track," Mrs. Boudreau declared. Then she added, "That's a hint. Simon?"

Simon scowled. He turned just enough to glance Meg's way. But she couldn't help him. She shook her head ever so slightly.

Mrs. Boudreau said, "That's right, Meg. Tend to your own business, and let Simon speak for himself." After a pause she went on. "We've already talked about this. It's been on the radio. Think," she urged, "beyond your own small world."

Simon made a stab at an answer. "The World Series? That's been on the radio."

A few kids giggled. Mrs. Boudreau whipped around and strode to the blackboard. With strokes so brisk she broke the chalk, she wrote: "DECLARATION OF INDEPENDENCE." Then beneath that she added, "BILL OF RIGHTS."

"Oh," Cindy Barter exclaimed, waving her hand in the air. "I know, I know."

"Well, go ahead then," Mrs. Boudreau told her. "Unless," she added, "I've shaken Simon's memory enough for him to come up with the right answer."

Simon stared at the blackboard as if it could yield just one more crucial hint.

"All right, Cindy."

"The Freedom Train!" Cindy declared.

Oh, that, thought Meg. At least now she could see that Mrs. Boudreau had made a joke when she'd mentioned getting back on track.

Nathan Mills raised his hand and asked whether it was the Yankees or the Dodgers that were coming on the Freedom Train, and where would it stop.

So Mrs. Boudreau had to go over what she had already told them about the special train that was traveling all around the country carrying famous documents from history. That was why they were about to learn something about them in school.

Meg and Simon exchanged looks. "American Revolution," she whispered as Mrs. Boudreau turned to the blackboard.

19

Meg glanced at the clock at the back of the room. At least there wouldn't be time for a test.

At recess the younger kids came in while grades four through six went out. Paul, his face beet red, was one of the last inside. Meg stopped him. "What happened?" she demanded.

"Nothing," he retorted, blinking back tears.

"You, Joan," Meg called into Miss Wylie's room. She saw Joan turn and then pretend not to hear. "See you later," Meg said in what she hoped was a menacing tone.

"Don't," Paul shouted. "Meg, don't."

"Well, what happened?" Meg insisted. "Just tell me. I won't do anything. Unless you want me to."

Paul hung back from the door to his room. "We were talking about what we would save in case of a fire. Miss Wylie told us to think about what mattered most to us."

"So?" prompted Meg.

"So we had to say our first choice out loud. Mine was the house flowers. Miss Wylie said house flowers might be a good third choice, but not first, since they could always be grown again with new seed. When I told her the house flowers were my banty hens, everyone laughed. Even though lots of kids said their dog or cat was what they'd save. It was because I called Grace and Disgrace house flowers that the kids made fun of them. At recess they squawked at me."

"All the kids?"

"Joan and her friends. But don't you go after her, Meg. You just make it worse." Paul darted into his room.

Meg slowly made her way out to the yard. She was thinking about what she would save from her own house first. And second, and third. The framed picture of Champ taken after he finished basic training? But Aunt Helen and Uncle Frank would save that. So what else?

Joyce Leblanc called to Meg. "You playing?"

Meg nodded. But by the time she joined the other kids she couldn't shake the gripping question about what was most precious to her. So she put it to them, and it had the same effect, bringing them up short, making them forget the softball game they usually played during recess.

"Things or people?" Skip Veazie asked.

"Not people. They'd be taken care of."

Dogs were mentioned. Cindy said she would take the dress she was going to wear at her aunt's wedding. Simon said he'd take his shotgun. Bobby Burrows said it wasn't really Simon's, not yet. Food, someone else declared. A flashlight, another put in. Blankets. Boots. The sheepskin hearth rug.

Everyone named something, even a new washing machine with a glass window in the door.

But Meg was stumped. She decided to look around when she got home. Would she have to confine herself to the back house, or could she consider some of the things in the big house that might belong to the Grays and Yeadons together? She didn't even have a clue to which things were jointly owned. Something like the china cabinet was simply a part of the household landscape she had always known.

Maybe Mom or Dad would have some ideas. One way or another she would figure out what mattered the most.

7 But after school Mom was still at work and Dad was out plowing the field below the barn. Uncle Frank thought it was a waste of time because the soil was too dry to hold furrows. Still, he admitted that the plowed field might be a good place to turn out the cows if a fire threatened, since there would be no stubble left in it to burn.

The field ran all the way down to the woods and extended uphill between the house and the barn. Dad plowed this section last. It was dark before he finished.

By the time he came in and washed up, supper was ready. At the table Uncle Frank talked about going to town tomorrow for extra water. There was a tank set up beside the war memorial on the town green where residents could help themselves to water. Dad, who had just plowed around the springhouse and checked the water level, agreed that it would be a good idea to fill a few milk cans and barrels while the town supply lasted.

When the door opened, Meg expected to see her mother coming in. But it wasn't Mom. It was Orin. He stood in the kitchen doorway, his face grimy, his fair hair stiff with filth, his arms held away from his body.

"Orin!" Gran exclaimed. "You're a sight!"

He seemed to Meg to have grown during the last few days. Even stooped with exhaustion, he almost filled the doorway. But that was often the impression he made, as if he were too big for any space he occupied.

"Didn't look for you to be home yet." This was Uncle Frank's greeting.

"Here to stay?" Aunt Helen asked as she moved toward him.

Orin shook his head. "Just tonight. To sleep."

"Well, get those things off," Aunt Helen told him. "We'll heat some water." She led him through to the bathroom as she spoke.

A few minutes later she returned with Orin's shirt, which was riddled with holes and scorch marks where embers had landed on his shoulders and arms. She held it up for everyone to see.

Paul stared and stared. "Was Orin on fire?" he asked.

"No," Dad said. "You just saw him. He's fine."

"Is he going to eat?" Paul went on.

"I surely hope so," Gran told him.

But when Aunt Helen went to check on Orin, she found him sound asleep in the bathtub in a couple of inches of tepid water. "He's wore out," she reported to the others.

"Let him be then," said Uncle Frank.

But by now Orin was roused. He wanted his supper. He came to the table in clean pants and shirt, but barefoot. Soot still blackened the creases around his eyes.

"What happened to your eyebrows?" Paul asked him.

Orin, his mouth full of beans, grinned at his little cousin.

"What happened?" Paul repeated.

"They got singed," Gran answered for Orin. Then she added, "I hope you're taking care." She came behind Orin and rested her hands on his shoulders. She looked over his head at Uncle Frank. "I don't like him getting that close to the fire."

Uncle Frank frowned. "Not now," he told her, signaling with an upraised hand. This brought on one of those silences that made no sense to Meg. Why shouldn't Gran be concerned for Orin's safety? For that matter, why shouldn't they all be worried? And what was wrong with saying so, especially when they all knew that Orin's reaction time wasn't quick? But Uncle Frank was shaking his head at Gran. He didn't want her to say any more about it.

After a moment Meg's father said, "Do they have you digging trenches, or what?"

Orin nodded. "Some. They're looking to get bulldozers. We knock out the ground fires, too. There's not enough water tanks." He wiped his plate with a slab of bread and stuffed it into his mouth.

"Lose any buildings?" asked Gran, who had returned to her chair.

Orin grunted. After swallowing, he said, "Chickens. Chicken farm burned. Everything."

Paul said, "If we had a fire here, I'd make the house flowers fly away."

"There's bird hunters around now," Uncle Frank warned him. "You let those banties fly into the woods and some trigger-happy fool's going to pop 'em."

Looking for confirmation, Paul turned to his father, who said, "Frank's right. Keep them close to home now."

"Stick them in the chicken coop," Aunt Helen said. "Get them used to being with the regular hens."

Dad shook his head. "They wouldn't last the night in there."

Orin slumped forward, his face in his plate, one arm sprawled. A fork clattered to the floor.

"Get that poor boy into bed," Gran ordered.

The two men rose and came around the table to sit Orin up. As they dragged him from the kitchen and hauled him up the stairs, Gran and Aunt Helen cleared away the mess he had made.

Paul went outside. Soon Meg heard him banging the pie tin. Almost at once the two little hens shot into the kitchen uttering plaintive chick sounds. Aunt Helen looked disgusted. "Useless things," she muttered.

"They did lay some eggs this summer," Meg reminded her.

"Tiny enough to fit in a teaspoon," Aunt Helen retorted.

"Never mind," Gran remarked. "Consider them ornaments." She brushed a few crumbs to the floor. "They please us," she declared as the hens scooted over to pick up the tidbits. "That's their use."

When the banties had cleaned up the last of the crumbs, Gran nodded to Paul, who scooped up his house flowers and carried them to their cage for the night.

Dad and Uncle Frank came downstairs. Dad said that Orin had some nasty burns on his ankles. Frank added that they didn't seem to bother Orin too much. He never did feel pain like most people.

"Still, Frank"—Dad chose his words with care—"if Orin's

going back to Croyden, shouldn't he wear some boots for protection?"

Gran nodded, wiping her hands on a dish towel. "Frank, you go look in your father's trunk. His barn boots are there. I cleaned them good and wrapped them in newspaper. They ought to fit the boy."

While Uncle Frank went about outfitting Orin for more fire fighting, Gran and Aunt Helen cleaned his burns with peroxide and smeared them with Unguentine. Through it all, Orin slept on, unaware.

8 When Meg got up the next morning, Dad was already gone. But Orin was still there, back from helping his father with the milking.

"You supposed to meet someone?" Aunt Helen asked him. "Or are they stopping for you here?"

Orin shrugged. He leaned over to untie his laces.

"Well, they must've said," she insisted.

"I don't know, Ma," Orin replied.

Gran said, "Call Ida. She'll know."

Sighing, Aunt Helen went to the telephone.

"What are you doing with those boots?" Gran asked Orin. "Don't they fit?"

"I don't want to wear them."

"They're your grampa's," Gran pointed out.

"I know," Orin told her. "That's why."

Gran went over to Orin and drew up a chair beside him. She could always tell when something spooked him. "Make you feel more than somewhat?" she asked him.

Orin nodded. He was used to Gran's old-fashioned way with words.

Gran said, "Your grampa would be proud to know you're helping like a man. He'd be proud of you, Orin. He'd like you to dress your feet in his boots."

"But . . . I can . . . smell him."

Gran put her hand on Orin's arm. In the parlor Aunt Helen spoke first with one neighbor, then with another. Everyone on the party line seemed to have picked up for this first call of the day. Gran said, "I can smell him, too, now you mention it. A good smell. It's all right, old son." She went on. "All right and right."

Orin sat there with his boots half unlaced. He didn't look at Gran, but Meg could tell that he had let her words in. Old son was what Grampa used to call Uncle Frank and Frank used to call Champ. Now Gran had said those words to Orin. Old son.

Aunt Helen rejoined them. "Start anytime," she told Orin. "Eddie's just out the door now."

Orin rose. Gran handed him a bag of sandwiches. "Anything to drink?" he asked. "Coke or anything?"

"Only milk," Aunt Helen told him.

"I'll take some. It's thirsty work."

Gran took a glass jar from the refrigerator. "Don't break it," she warned.

"No," Orin responded. He headed for the door.

"Take care," Gran called after him.

"Yes, be careful," Aunt Helen said.

"Yup," he answered as the door slammed behind him.

Meg darted out after him. "Orin, wait," she called. "I have to ask you something."

He stopped. "You take the horses for a drink tomorrow," he told her.

Meg said, "Uncle Frank doesn't want them using water for the cows."

"You take them," Orin insisted.

And how would she manage that without being seen? Two big draft horses were hard to conceal. But this was one of those times when Orin expected her to obey him just the way both of them had always obeyed Champ. "Yes, okay," she said, granting him the authority of age. "Orin," she added, "if we had a fire here, what would you want to save?"

Orin half turned. He seemed to be examining the lumber stacked across the driveway, set aside for Meg's family's own house, which was to be built next spring. "Them," Orin said. "Toby and June."

"Well, of course we'd save the horses. But what else? From the house."

Orin shrugged. "Dunno. Nothing heavy. With all the smoke, you don't carry heavy things. Can't breathe."

"Things to go in the truck," Meg explained. "Think of what you'd want."

"My shoes," he finally declared. "My own shoes. The radio." He paused. "My good ax. My moose horn. My leather jacket."

"It's all torn."

"You asked. My jacket and Champ's fishing rod."

He was on his way again. Meg called after him to tie his boot laces. But he went along to the road with them open at the ankles. Meg figured maybe the burns were bothering him after all, enough to prevent him from lacing the boots up tight.

9 By Friday it was clear that the Croyden fire was out of control. On the radio it was compared to the fire along the new turnpike, which had been contained time and again but still kept cropping up. Everything seemed to hinge on the wind, which kept shifting. The fact that the fire could generate its own wind only confused the matter. No one dared predict where the fire was heading.

In school the kids discussed wind direction as if they knew what they were talking about. Simon said his uncle was sending all his cattle away as soon as he could arrange for a livestock trailer to haul them.

"Away where?" asked Bobby Burrows. "My father can't find a farm that can take ours. We've got thirty-seven milking."

"I don't know," Simon answered, "but my uncle's right close to Croyden. He worked out a deal over to Marks Mills. Your father could find out the name from mine."

Mrs. Boudreau said the state was taking over the situation. All woods were closed now, although hunting was still allowed in open land and marshes. Equipment was being rushed from as far away as Boston. Civil Air Patrol planes had been called in to help track new outbreaks of fire.

"Maybe our school will burn," Simon whispered to Meg. "I heard on the radio that fire can take one house and go right past another that's next to it. What if—"

"This is not a time for private conversations," said Mrs. Boudreau. "Do you want to share something with all of us, Simon?"

Simon straightened. "I was wondering what would happen if the fire came near here. I mean, the younger kids might panic."

Meg was filled with admiration. Simon could always talk his way out of a corner.

Mrs. Boudreau said she was glad that he was thinking ahead. She and Miss Wylie had already considered how they would evacuate the school, if it came to that.

Hands shot up. Questions came from all around the room. Mrs. Boudreau kept assuring everyone that as of now no one in Charity Corners was in immediate danger.

Still, the questions kept coming. Obviously some families

had passed on their nervousness to their children. But most of the kids just wanted to find out how they could get near enough to the fire to see some action. At recess they didn't even bother to get a game going. They just stood around telling one another what they would do in an emergency.

"It could happen anywhere," Nathan maintained. "Some fires burn underground for days and then suddenly come up through the roots of trees."

"First off," said Bobby, "I'd look for someone that needed to be rescued."

"What about hunting down the guy that started the fire?" Simon suggested.

Meg listened to the boys scheme about how they would hide off the road to catch the firebug.

"You'd be a lot smarter going for the fire warden," Cindy pointed out. "Your firebug's probably twice your size."

"There wouldn't be time," Simon told her. "The firebug would be long gone."

"Or any grown-up," Cindy went on.

"They'd all be busy," Skip said. "They'd be fighting the fire somewhere else."

"So you'd tackle the guy," Joyce remarked, "and then he'd pick himself up and drive away."

"Still," Simon retorted, "it would teach him a lesson. We ought to do it this weekend," he proposed. "Patrol the camps around Charity Pond. Hunters from away always move in on those cabins."

Skip didn't think his family would let him out of sight this weekend, but Simon and Bobby and Nathan were pretty sure they could get away for a few hours. Meg and Joyce exchanged a look. They had no intention of letting the boys go out to Charity Pond without them.

Later Meg made Simon promise to call her as soon as they decided when and where they were meeting.

"If it stays this hot," Simon told her, "maybe we can jump in the pond, too."

That did it for Meg. She wasn't about to be left behind, not with the prospect of a swim, too. Think of swimming in the middle of October!

10 Mom was back but sleeping when Meg and Paul came home. Meg had to run after Paul to keep him from going into Mom's room.

"I wasn't going to wake her," he protested. "I just wanted to look."

"You'll see her when she gets up," Meg told him. But she knew exactly how he felt. It made all the difference just knowing Mom was there.

"Go help Gran," Aunt Helen suggested. "It'll make the time go by."

"Doing what?" Paul asked guardedly.

"She's in the attic. Looking for what to save."

"Why?"

"Just in case. Lots of people are doing it now, loading up."

So Meg and Paul climbed up the steep attic stairs. They found Gran huddled over an open trunk. Old-fashioned pictures adorned the paper that lined the inside of the top. But Gran wasn't looking at the pictures; she was turning over some yellowed cloth.

"What's that?" Paul asked.

"My wedding dress," Gran replied, setting it aside to pull out some other material beneath it.

"Should I carry the wedding dress downstairs?" asked Meg, who couldn't wait to spread it out on a bed.

Gran shook her head. "There's no need of it now. But this

30

one," she went on, placing the folded fabric in Meg's arms, "is some of my mother's homespun. Good stuff."

"Where should I put it?" Meg asked her.

"In my room. I'll have to sort through everything again."

Meg carried the material, which smelled of camphor and was scratchy on her skin. It wasn't even a nice color, sort of reddish brown. She couldn't imagine any use for it.

On her way back up, she met Paul staggering under a small rolled rug. Taking it from him, she dropped it beside the homespun. By the time she returned to the attic the trunk was shut and Gran was poring through a box of old pictures and letters. It was so dim up here that Meg could barely make out the images that held Gran spellbound.

"I'm going down," Paul said.

"That's right," Gran told him. "Get some sunshine while you can."

Sunshine? thought Meg. Didn't Gran realize that everyone was praying for clouds and rain?

From between the pages of an old photograph album Gran extracted something that at first glance looked to Meg like a drawing on a sheet of paper. Gran smoothed it out. It wasn't paper after all, but a piece of cloth. The picture was stitched with faded colored threads. Meg peered closely. It was almost exactly like the farmhouse, except that there was a barn at the end.

"I was younger than you when I made this sampler," Gran said. "Before the Grays took down the old barn. Your great-grandfathers, both of them, wanted the cows downhill by the spring. That was some do, that move, and all the building. My mother said, 'Never again.' But years later her house, the house I grew up in, was moved down the road. By then I was married and living here, and she came to spend her last years under this roof. She never quite settled, not in her heart. I guess I understand now. I can't imagine being anywhere else." She pointed to the tree pictured in the sampler in front of the cross-stitched house. "That's your swing tree," she said.

"What happened to your first house?" asked Meg. "Where did it get moved to?"

"Just down the road. I told you. Where the Leblancs are."

"Joyce's house was yours?" Meg exclaimed.

Gran nodded as she folded the sampler. "It hadn't far to go. We lived just beyond the orchard. Even then we had apple trees all around. The first sampler I ever made was of that house. I had such a good time stitching in the apples that when I stitched this sampler, I went and turned the maple here into an apple tree, too. But my mother made me take out all those little red apples and fix the tree to be true."

Slowly Gran worked her way through the attic clutter. Down under the eaves she had to walk almost doubled over to avoid the roofing nails that stuck through. When Meg straightened too suddenly, it felt as if she had bumped her head into a coil of barbed wire.

"Will we have to put all this stuff back?" she asked after lugging a spinning wheel treadle down to Gran's room and setting it beside an old wooden churn.

Gran leaned back with a sigh. "I expect." She handed over a brown jug with a chipped spout. "Careful. It's heavier than it looks."

"It's broken," Meg said. "So why save it?" By now Gran's room and the upstairs hall were crammed with things that looked to Meg like junk.

"I recollect it full of buttermilk. Your great-grandmother told me it was as old as this house."

"Will there be room for everything?" Meg asked. "Where will we take it all?"

"With us," Gran replied. "And then, if we're lucky, right back home again. If home still stands."

"But just in case," Meg suggested, "maybe you should look over what we've already brought down from the attic."

Gran nodded and heaved herself forward. She was ready for a rest.

She had to take the stairs sideways like a child whose legs are too short for the steps. She was nearly down when Meg's mother appeared in the upstairs hall.

"Ma, what on earth are you up to?" she demanded as she reached for Gran's hand.

"I thought you were catching up on your sleep," Gran told her, adding, "Don't worry, Lil, we won't take all this. I still have the cellar to do. I'm not leaving my preserves behind, no matter what."

Mom just groaned.

11 Mom and Meg fetched and carried while Gran sorted and resorted. Finally Mom shook her head at the impossibility of it all. She said, "I wonder if this is necessary. With volunteers pouring in to fight the fires, it's hard to believe we're in more danger than we've always been, considering."

"Considering what?" asked Meg.

A look passed between Gran and Mom.

"What?" demanded Meg.

"Come on downstairs," Mom said to her. "Gran wants to putter around here without us bothering her."

Meg followed her mother down through the kitchen and on into the little house to her bedroom. When the door was closed, Mom said, "Fire's always been a danger, especially before we got in the electricity."

"When was that?" Meg had a vague memory of hurricane lamps in every room. Now there were lightbulbs with pull strings to turn them on.

Mom sank down on the bed. "Let's see. I was carrying Paul. We'd put it off, the electricity. Your grandfather was still alive, and he was used to the old way. But with another baby coming . . . there were safety reasons."

Something else was going on, something Mom didn't want Meg to know. "Why safety reasons?" she asked.

"Well," Mom answered, "just imagine milking by lamplight. Think how the wind shoots through the barn when the door at the end is open. Think of the hay."

"Was there a fire in the barn once?"

"You know what?" Mom declared. "Fire is not my favorite subject right now. I have most of the weekend off, but after that I may not get home for a while. Because of this fire crisis. They've asked Nancy and me to stay on duty at the exchange."

"And not come home at all?" It was bad enough having Mom away as much as she was. If only Aunt Helen still worked at the shoe factory in Marks Mills, then Mom would have to stay home. But of course Aunt Helen and Uncle Frank weren't trying to save up enough money to build a house. Besides, even if Aunt Helen went back to work, Gran would still be here to look after things at the farm.

As if Mom could read Meg's thoughts, she tried to reassure her. "Dad will be here. And the others."

"Where will you sleep?" Meg asked her.

"There's a cot upstairs for us. Don't worry. And plenty of food and blankets. Anyway, it's too hot up there for blankets." Mom meant at the telephone exchange up over the hardware store. "You be good," Mom told her. "Help out with Paul."

"When I do, everyone tells me to mind my own business."

"That doesn't mean getting into fights like you always used to over Orin."

"Well, Orin's family, too," Meg retorted. "Isn't my own family my business? Anyway, what's it got to do with Orin? Why were you and Gran looking at each other that way? It's about him, isn't it?"

Mom frowned. She held her arms out to Meg, who crawled into them, feeling too big for Mom's lap but wishing she could still be cuddled the way Paul sometimes was.

"It's tricky," Mom finally responded. "I guess you're old enough to hear this, but you're not to mention it. I don't want Paul getting wind of it."

Meg nodded against her mother's bony chest. How different Mom and Aunt Helen were. Even though Aunt Helen looked like the kind of mother who would snuggle with her children, Meg couldn't remember ever seeing her hug Orin. And of course Champ was way too old for cuddling, at least as far back as Meg could recall.

"A long time ago," Mom said, her voice low, "when Orin was little, he was drawn to fire. It was bad, like fire just took him over. From the start we had no idea what was wrong. Like when he was a baby and cried so much. And banged his head. You couldn't get him to smile at you. And when you held him, even his own mother, he'd arch his back and hold himself off. It was almost like he was fighting us when we tried to comfort him. Sometimes we couldn't even be sure he heard us." Mom paused. "When he was, I don't know, three or so, he took a shingle and used it like a torch. The curtains burned, a few other things."

Meg straightened up. "The curtains? Is that all? Why is it a secret?" Then more came to her. "Is that why Uncle Frank gets so mad about people setting fires? Because of Orin? Did he get mad when the curtains burned up?"

"Orin meant no harm. He was only a baby then."

"Why didn't you tell me before?" Meg demanded. "Why can't Paul know?"

Mom shook her head. "Because it would be that much harder for Orin. If people found out, they'd be afraid of him. He'd never get work. Anyway," Mom added, "that's how Frank and Helen wanted to handle it. Where Orin's concerned, Frank's always believed the less said the better."

Meg mulled this over. "Better for Orin," she said, "or for Aunt Helen and Uncle Frank?"

"Now don't you be fresh, Meg," Mom retorted. "You can't begin to understand what they've been through. From the time Orin was born. You can't know. No one can."

Meg wanted to insist that she knew a deal more than outsiders. After all, she and Orin were more like sister and brother than cousins. But the truth was that she had never fully realized how different Orin was until she started school. She had only seen that Aunt Helen and Uncle Frank favored Champ, who was quick and clever and handsome. Was that what had made Champ and Gran act so fiercely loyal to Orin? Meg supposed that she had always sensed that they were trying to make it up to him.

Then how did this fire thing fit into everything else that set Orin apart? It only seemed to help explain Uncle Frank. She said, "Uncle Frank says that whoever starts a fire is like a murderer."

When Mom didn't reply, Meg went on. "Orin isn't a murderer, is he?"

"No," Mom said. "But there were a few more incidents, close calls. It was a worry. It took a long time for him to learn to control himself."

"Now he's helping put out fires," Meg said. "That should make everyone glad."

Mom nodded. "But after all the scares, all the trouble, and with Champ being killed, it seems like all Frank and Helen can see is what's lost. When it comes to Orin, they mostly notice what's wrong with him, not what's right."

"Right like what?" Meg asked.

"Like how good-hearted he is. How strong and hardworking. And he does keep learning."

"How come he didn't in school?"

"That's a different kind of learning," Mom told her.

Meg nodded. That made sense to her. She was glad that at least some of the family could see more in Orin than that he was Champ's backward brother.

"I wish you wouldn't stay in town," Meg said.

"I know," Mom answered. "But I'll be home before you know it."

12 Saturday morning was so hectic that Meg forgot all about meeting Simon and the other kids at Charity Pond. For one thing, all the furniture was being moved around. For another, there was a change in the air. The sky, relentlessly blue for so many weeks, had turned dingy gray with a dull orange smear on the northwest horizon. A faint scent of smoke drifted over the farm.

"No sign of fire, though," Aunt Helen remarked. "Not even smoke that you can see."

Standing in the dooryard, Gran scanned the fields and pastures and the woodlot past the plowed field below the barn. She shook her head. "I don't like it. Let's get the truck loaded."

"Time enough for that, Ma," Uncle Frank told her. "We should get water around the house in case we have to wet down the roof and the clapboards that are close to the ground. Same goes for the barn."

Then the phone rang. It was Simon calling to say they would meet at Miss Trilling's boat landing. Meg reminded him that they weren't allowed there.

"We won't go near the lodge or anything," Simon assured her. "It's just a place to meet."

Meg went out to ask her mother if she could go.

"You know I don't like you swimming with no one in charge," Mom said.

"We'll stick together," Meg promised. "We all know how to swim."

"Oh, let her go," Gran urged. "The kids need something to do on a day like this."

Meg raced into the house, got into her bathing suit with her dungarees over it, then went to get Champ's bike out of the back house. In her haste she stumbled over the house flowers, who set off squawks of alarm and flew outside into the morning haze.

"Grace!" Paul called. "Disgrace! You stay here." Crooning to the hens, he walked over to the swing. They scuttled after him, leaped into his lap, and then flapped to keep their balance as he pushed and pumped skyward. He didn't even ask Meg where she was going on Champ's bike.

She swung into the seat that was too high for her, wobbling as she started off. By the time she reached Alder Swamp Road she was covered with dust and sweat and thinking only of plunging into the water. Then she passed the place where the fire must have started. She stared at what was left of the trees. She couldn't help liking the smell of the scorched wood. It made her wonder about Orin. What exactly did Mom mean? Wasn't everyone drawn to fire? Meg loved to gaze into flames on cold, dark nights. Was that what it was like for Orin? There had to be more than that to it if it made him do such dangerous things. Then what was it like for him to douse a fire that at a younger age he might have set? Didn't he know how dangerous it was?

Standing up to pedal harder, she cast back in her mind over Champ's especially dangerous stunts. She was looking for one that had involved Orin. Like the time Champ decided to teach him to drive. As usual Champ had brought her along, making her an accomplice and swearing her to secrecy. Even now, after more than three years, her stomach heaved at the thought of that lesson.

Champ had often used the car when his mother didn't need it to get to the shoe factory. This time at least he had had the sense to take it into a distant field before he changed places with Orin. At first nothing much had happened, except a lot of lurching that flung Meg off the backseat onto the floor. Each time Orin stalled the car, she had prayed that the lesson was over. But Champ had egged him on until finally Orin had the car hurtling wildly over the rough ground. While Meg had clung for dear life to the back of the front seat, Champ had cheered and occasionally grabbed at the steering wheel to swing them away from a tree or a stone wall.

At the time Meg had felt certain that Orin must have been as terrified as she was. But when, unable to stop, he finally slammed into a haystack, where the car mercifully stalled, he had seemed barely aware of how close he had come to wrecking the car and killing all three of them. Champ's shrill laughter had actually coaxed a smile out of him. In the end it seemed that all that had mattered was pleasing Champ.

Not that Orin spoke out about his feelings. Meg couldn't remember one single time when he had looked her in the eye and said or showed what was in his heart. Not even when Champ was killed. Not directly, anyway.

Wheeling onto the turnoff to Charity Pond, Meg scudded along until she came to Miss Trilling's gateposts. She left the bike there and walked down between the lodge and the carriage house and stable. On the boat landing Bobby was skipping stones and Simon was sitting with his pants rolled up, his bare feet dangling in the water. It wasn't long before other kids arrived. They gazed out over the pond. Leaves still brilliant from the late-fall turning floated at the water's edge, but there was a dullness to the light; it spread more gloom than color.

They decided to split up into teams. Meg and Simon and Bobby would inspect the three cabins at the north end of the pond. The others would check out the cabins that fronted the pond to the south and east of the lodge.

As Meg's team returned to Miss Trilling's driveway, Simon halted. "While we're here," he said, "it can't hurt to look."

Meg shook her head. "There's nothing to see. You've seen it before."

"Are those screens still on?"

Meg nodded. "They leave them because they don't want the paint to shake off."

Simon said, "I'll just be a second."

Bobby shouted, "Wait up," and sprinted after him.

"Don't you touch a thing," Meg yelled after them. Any grown-up coming along now would think she was keeping watch for the boys. Not that she expected anyone to show up. Dad was the only likely person, since he was supposed to keep an eye on the place.

Meg loved coming here with him, even if it was to help unload hay into the loft. She especially loved coming when Miss Trilling was at home. Her cook would bring out lemonade and cookies. It felt like being in a movie. Dad always stood, because hayseed stuck all over him and he had been taught by his father to keep a respectful distance here. But Meg would head straight for the wrought-iron love seat next to the table set with frosted glasses and the plate of delicate cookies dusted with powdered sugar. She would nibble the cookies to make them last. Dad always told her to shake a leg; he always seemed uncomfortable here.

Two summers ago, when Meg scraped her arm in the hayloft, the cook had taken her inside to wash off the blood and hayseed. Meg had stalled as long as she could and had got as far as the pantry while the cook went looking for a Band-Aid. Meg had never seen so much china. There was one whole shelf of soup tureens and covered serving dishes. She had managed a peek through to the dining room, too, where she had glimpsed the polished sideboard and the heads of animals adorning the wall. But that was the farthest she had ever penetrated the lodge.

Everyone hereabouts knew that Miss Trilling's grandfather had built the place about a hundred years ago as a rustic summer retreat. It had been copied from a famous hunting lodge in Europe. Certainly no one in Prescott Falls had ever seen anything remotely like it. While summer visitors from New York and Florida might come and go, the lodge remained a mystery to almost everyone else. Except for Meg's father and Mr. Bowden, the plumber, no one ever got a look inside. Not even Mrs. Bowden knew much about the place since all Mr. Bowden ever seemed to notice were bathroom fixtures and pipes.

Just as Meg was beginning to wonder what was keeping the boys, they came tearing toward her. She asked them whether they'd seen a ghost.

Bobby nodded. Simon said, "Not exactly."

Meg started to laugh.

"No kidding," Bobby told her. "Someone's in there."

Meg shook her head. "It's all locked up for the winter."

"See for yourself then."

They ran back together, but when they neared the lodge, Meg slowed. Her father's warnings resounded in her head: no running, no yelling, no fooling around.

The boys were quiet, too. Gesturing, they led Meg to a side window. Here was the screen with the picture of a waterfall and a stone arch in the foreground. The trees painted on the screen were green and lush, nothing like the real trees around the lodge. Meg knew, as everyone did, that the painted screens worked like one-way blinds to keep the inside of the house private. From indoors the view out was clear.

"There's nothing to see but the pictures," Meg said.

"Ssh," whispered Simon.

They waited in silence.

Something like a shadow passed behind the screen. Or was Meg imagining it? There wasn't a sound from the house, but the shadowy change came again, right there behind the painted waterfall, a dark blot followed by light.

Meg backed away. Something inside had moved. Or someone. Was the someone looking out at three kids staring at the shifting image on the screen?

Meg retreated. The boys came with her. In hushed tones they considered what might be inside. Hunters sometimes broke into cabins on the pond. Usually they helped themselves to shelter and a bed with blankets, seldom leaving a mess. But who would break into the lodge, which was sealed like a fortress? A robber wouldn't stay there, would he? And what could he steal without a truck to carry away his loot?

Meg said she would tell her father so that he could check the place. Meanwhile, she reminded the boys, they were supposed to be doing some checking of their own along the north shore.

So they took off, making plenty of noise now as they trampled brittle branches and dry vegetation. Anyone around the cabins could have heard them coming and would have had plenty of time to get lost. Still, they knew there would be telltale signs left behind. The smell of burning from one of the outdoor fireplaces, for instance.

It didn't occur to them that they were already growing accustomed to breathing smoky air.

13 They spent a long time tracking down false leads. Again and again bridle paths and trails returned them to their starting point.

By midafternoon they were hot and hungry. And discouraged. They took time out for a swim, which felt so good it almost made up for failing to find a firebug. Later, drying in the smoky haze that filtered through the trees, they talked about going back to the lodge and taking by surprise the person lurking inside.

"Maybe it's not a human," Bobby said. "It could be a bear."

Simon shook his head. "We'd've seen where it got in."

"A spy could get in," Bobby countered, "and we'd never know how."

"There's only spies during a war," Meg said. "The war's been over for two years."

"So where did all the spies go?" Bobby demanded. "I bet some of them are still hiding out."

All three of them could remember the warnings about possible spies along the coast who might send signals to German submarines. Was Charity Pond close enough to the coast to harbor a leftover spy?

Then Simon came up with another idea. Maybe the person in the lodge was an escaped prisoner of war.

Meg sucked in her breath. Think of that. What if he didn't speak English?

"Weren't they all sent back?" asked Bobby.

"Probably," Simon responded. "Maybe this guy escaped before the war ended and he's been on the run ever since."

Meg told them to stay away from the lodge. If there was a spy or a prisoner inside, they'd only make him nervous poking around. Then he'd get away before her father could come with his key and walk right in.

The boys agreed, but they didn't think it was fair for Meg to be the only one of them on hand for the arrest. "Don't tell your father or anyone else until Monday after school. Then we'll be waiting out on the road and you can make him stop and pick us up."

"He might not want to," Meg said.

"He'll have to. You'll tell him we're the ones that found the guy."

Meg nodded. She didn't try to explain that her father wasn't likely to take orders from her. And how could she explain trespassing there in the first place? Snooping, Dad would call it. Absolutely forbidden.

Simon and Bobby were satisfied. So the day wasn't a total loss. Besides, they had had a swim.

Starting back on their bikes, they met Joyce and Nathan on Alder Swamp Road. After the boys turned up Chimney Hill, Meg and Joyce went on together. Meg had to stop herself from telling Joyce about the mysterious presence in the lodge. Meg wished she hadn't promised to keep it a secret. But Dad mustn't find out from anyone else that she and the boys had been spying at Miss Trilling's window.

Joyce invited Meg to stop in at her house, but halfway up the driveway they halted. Champ's bike fell over. Ignoring it, the girls just stood there. Joyce's father was on his tractor, plowing a trench around the house. Gran's house, Meg thought, suddenly wondering what had become of the sampler with the apple trees on it.

Slowly the girls walked toward the door. A shovel lay across the front steps. Joyce's mother waved them back. The tractor was coming around again. Joyce's mother explained that all this mess was to save the house if the fire came. She said that Joyce's dad would lay some planks to the door when he finished digging his ditch.

Meg decided to go on home. Walking her bike to the road, she hiked herself up on it. She glanced back, trying to picture this house as Gran had described it with apple trees in its yard. But all she saw was Joyce's home surrounded by a moat of raw earth. The picture she sought was inside Gran's head and maybe on a sampler cross-stitched long ago by a child's hand. She pedaled hard, anxious to find out whether her own dooryard was torn up, too.

She found the farmhouse intact, the truck and hay wagon pulled up close, one behind the other. Dad and Uncle Frank were loading the sofa onto the truck. Meg's mother and Aunt Helen emerged from the house, carrying Gran's wicker rocking chair.

Paul watched from the swing. "They took the china cupboard," he told Meg. "I'm watching to be sure they don't take my bed."

Seeing the hay wagon reminded Meg of the horses. "Did anyone take Toby and June for a drink today?" she asked Paul. When he said he didn't know, she called to her mother, "Anyone water the horses today?"

Mom shrugged. She wasn't thinking about Toby and June.

Meg detoured to the barn for a lead rope and then took off for the orchard. At the barway she called the horses. They came so quickly she guessed they had been without water all day. That was because Uncle Frank was so worried about the cows, which needed plenty of water to produce milk. He figured he could cut back on water for the horses as long as they weren't working.

Meg had to stand on the stone wall to snap the rope on Toby's halter. Swatting him back, she lowered the bars. Zac came up behind her and helped slow the eager horses by weaving back and forth in front of them. Still, it was a little scary being in their way.

The water in the barnyard tank was low. The horses gulped noisily. Meg hoped they would finish before Uncle Frank caught sight of them there, but they kept their heads deep inside the trough, even their forelocks getting wet as they swished and slobbered and gulped some more.

She managed to get them back to the orchard without being noticed. She had already decided that if Uncle Frank caught her letting them drink the cows' water, she wouldn't tell him Orin had asked her to. Despite Gran's insistence that Orin wasn't Meg's responsibility, he still needed to be protected.

She looked around, as if Champ were just off to the side, somewhere nearby. See? she wanted to tell him as she slid the top bar into its slot. See? I'm looking after Orin like you said. Minding the horses for him. Keeping my promise.

14 They had an early supper Sunday because Dad had to drive Mom into Prescott Falls. Before she left, she had a serious talk with Meg and Paul. She asked them to find ways to be especially good and helpful.

"Like not taking a bath to save water?" Paul said.

Mom sighed. "You can have a small one, to be clean for school. Use Meg's water when she's done."

"I won't need a bath," Meg informed her. "I went swimming yesterday."

Mom frowned. She seemed about to speak but didn't. "Just be good," she repeated. "Pray for rain."

"Then all the furniture will get wet," Paul objected.

Mom said she could think of worse problems. Then she drew Meg and Paul close. "Now listen," she told them. "If they have to evacuate the school, just do exactly what Miss Wylie and Mrs. Boudreau say. Even if you're taken somewhere you don't know."

"And not try to get home?" Meg asked. "What about Gran and Aunt Helen?"

"I'm talking about if you're not already with them. The point is, someone will be in charge, to take care of you."

"If we go somewhere we don't know, how will you find us?" Paul asked her.

"All the calls come through the exchange, so I'll probably know where you are before you do."

Meg said, "Joyce's father dug a hole all around their house. Are we going to do that, too?"

"How did he?" Paul wanted to know.

"First he plowed. Then I think he was going to shovel."

Mom said, "Gran and Dad and Frank and Helen will decide what to do here. Oh, and I forgot. No more flushing. Use the privy from now on."

Dad came in and picked up Mom's suitcase. "Ready, Lil?" he asked.

Mom nodded. She hugged both children at once.

Suddenly Meg blurted, "Can't we come with you in the car?"

Straightening, Mom looked at Dad. He shrugged. Then Mom nodded.

Paul and Meg were out the door and racing to the car before their parents changed their minds.

Just past Charity Corners Dad slowed to have a look at Oxbow Stream. There was barely enough light to see the dark trickle that crazed around stones and rotted branches. Here and there the water seemed to vanish entirely, only to emerge again like some exhausted traveler struggling to cover the last mile home. There wasn't much stream left to flow into the river. Dad glanced up to the left, where darkness now

47

shrouded Chimney Hill. "Wouldn't want to depend on my well up there," he remarked, "if that's all the water coming down."

On they went, the railroad tracks to their right for a while, but no sound of a train. Here and there a barn loomed or a house sent out shafts of light from its windows. The darkness deepened.

When the car stopped jiggling, Meg could tell that they had reached the paved road, but she couldn't see it. A few cars with headlights beamed toward them. It seemed ages before they came to the mill outside Prescott Falls. At last Meg could make out some of the houses that lined the town green. She was even able to see one side of the war memorial that had Champ's name on it. Here was the town hall and the church. There was Libby's Market with the Esso gas pump out front and the big sign over the door proclaiming it a Nation-Wide Service Grocer. Dad pulled over at the hardware store. The central telephone office was upstairs.

He carried Mom's suitcase up the outside stairway and into the exchange. Mom followed. A moment later he returned to the car. He didn't speak.

Paul, half asleep, nodded in the corner of the backseat. Meg scrunched forward until she was right behind Dad. She hoped he would invite her to climb in front, but he didn't. The next thing she knew he was shaking her awake. Quietly he gathered up Paul and carried him to the house. It was so dark now that Meg nearly blundered into the wagon.

When they were inside, Dad finally spoke. "Go pull down the covers."

Meg ducked past him. As she picked up Paul's dump truck from the bed and pulled off the spread, it came to her that this time next year she would have her own room in the house that would be started in the spring. A house just for the four Yeadons. She didn't think she would miss living in the farmhouse. She didn't feel like Gran, who couldn't imagine being anywhere else. After all, thought Meg, she could still come back to spend some time with Gran whenever she felt like it.

15 The radio blared out the Monday morning fire news. Yesterday it had rained in Portland. Gran said that was a hopeful sign. Uncle Frank disagreed. After all, it had only been a shower; besides, yesterday's temperature had broken the heat record.

Meg paid close attention to the grown-ups' talk. She listened for the drift of things around the farm so that she could figure out how to get her father alone this afternoon to tell him about the person hiding out in Miss Trilling's lodge. If Gran overheard, she was bound to ask Meg whose business she had been tending that had taken her so close to the lodge. Meg figured that if she was very careful, she might get Dad to investigate before he began to wonder on his own what she had been up to.

Uncle Frank decided to go over to the Kreskys' in case Pete and Eddie needed help moving out their heavy equipment.

"But Eddie's with Orin," Meg reminded him.

Uncle Frank shrugged. "He could've come back."

"Without Orin?" Meg exclaimed. How could Orin be left in Croyden with strangers? Had Uncle Frank forgotten about him? At least Eddie Kresky sort of looked out for Orin. "Eddie wouldn't leave Orin behind," Meg said.

"I guess not," Uncle Frank replied.

Aunt Helen told Meg and Paul to get their school things. Uncle Frank would drive them to Charity Corners today.

"Can't we wait till we find out about Orin?" asked Meg.

49

"There's nothing to find out," Aunt Helen told her. "He'll be back as soon as he can, and then he'll tell you all about the fire."

"He won't," Paul said. "He never talks to us."

Aunt Helen thrust lunch boxes at the children. "You can ask him, though," she said. "He answers questions."

Uncle Frank let Meg and Paul ride in back on the sofa. Meg told Paul they were a king and queen carried on their throne on top of an elephant. But when they stopped to pick up Joyce, she said it looked more like one of those crazy rides at the Coventry Fair, only slower.

"Bouncier," Paul corrected.

Joyce hoped they would cause a stir coming to school like this, but hardly anyone noticed. Over the weekend some of the parents had taken their children to stay with relatives living safely away from the hot spots. School was only about half full.

It felt sort of creepy, but it also cranked up everyone's excitement and disrupted the normal routine. Both rooms joined forces for a fire drill that involved crawling around on the floor under towels that would be wet in a real emergency. The kids bumped into chairs and desks and then one another on purpose.

"Don't forget this afternoon," Simon whispered to Meg, and then he put his head down like a bull and butted her.

"This isn't a game," Mrs. Boudreau told them. "It could be a matter of life or death."

But the older kids could remember those very words from the air-raid drills they used to have when the war was still on. They had practiced keeping clear of windows with their hands behind their necks. After a while they knew the drill so well it got boring. Every time a plane flew overhead they would run to have a look. But nothing ever happened. And then the war was over. Since then the only excitement to hit

50

Charity Corners was Vernon Barter driving his truck out onto the ice and falling through. It had taken two tractors and a whole lot more chain than anyone would have guessed to haul that truck out of Charity Pond. Everyone this side of the river had come to watch.

So it was hard for the older kids to get all worked up over learning how to escape from a burning building. Besides, the girls had trouble tucking their skirts down close and had to be separated from the boys.

After a while Miss Wylie and Mrs. Boudreau pronounced the children as ready as they could be for what might come.

When they were all mixed up together again, Simon whispered to Meg that at least they had a real spy or prisoner of war to keep them on their toes.

They never did settle down to work. After lunch and recess Mrs. Boudreau let her students talk about what their families were doing to prepare for the worst. Most of them had loaded trucks and cars with their most valuable things, too. Not everyone had a refrigerator and washing machine. Even so, Nathan's father and grandfather had carted their icebox and washtub with its wringer into the middle of a plowed field because Nathan's mother said she could face anything except doing without them. It also turned out that other people besides Joyce's father were plowing trenches to make no-burn areas for keeping things safe.

By the time school let out, Meg could see dark clouds on the northern horizon. Mrs. Boudreau and Miss Wylie thought it might be raining in Croyden. But as the children started off for their homes, the clouds thickened to a single dark mass. Soon everyone could tell that what had seemed to be a cloud bank was smoke.

Meg tried to hurry Paul along, but he dawdled, walking in the dry ditch beside the road. He said he was looking for arrowheads.

Meg considered going on without him. Now was the time to speak to Dad. No matter how she told him about the person hiding out in the lodge, Dad might still be mad at her for invading Miss Trilling's privacy. Of course, Meg could say that she wasn't really doing that since Miss Trilling wasn't even there. But if she got into an argument with Dad, she would only make him madder. The important thing was to get him all stirred up about the real invader.

Just when she was about to take off, Dad's car came clattering up to them, almost lost in the dust it raised. He stopped to let Meg and Paul into the back and then lurched into gear.

"Dad," Meg said, "there's something I've got to tell you." But how to begin?

"There's something I've got to tell you, too," he said. "They're calling for more volunteers. I'm going right after milking. Bryce Leblanc and me."

"To Croyden?"

"No," Dad answered. "A new fire broke out east of town. Over toward Coventry. While the wind's out of the north, there's a chance we can stop it spreading through Prescott Falls."

"But there's something else you need to do," Meg blurted. "Something we found out—"

"That's enough, Meg." Dad sounded flustered. "Like it or not, you'll have to keep your opinion to yourself and let the grown-ups decide what needs doing."

"But, Dad—" She broke off as he swung around to fix her with a hard look. She had never seen him like this before. "Do you have to go right away?" she asked.

Dad nodded. "Almost. I expect you to do exactly what Gran and Aunt Helen tell you. They're thinking of taking you to Aunt Helen's folks in Lerwick."

"When's Mom coming home?" Paul asked him.

"I don't know, Paul. She's got an essential job to do. She knows you'll be taken out of here if it's necessary."

When the car turned into the driveway and stopped, Dad was out and striding down toward the barn before Meg and Paul could ask him anything else. Both of them sort of leaned against the front fender as if the car were an extension of their father.

"Who will deliver the mail?" Paul asked Meg.

"How should I know?" she snapped. Dad was going away. He was acting so strange that he seemed already distant. He certainly wasn't about to listen to anything she had to tell him, especially not about a shadow that moved behind Miss Trilling's fancy window screen. Spy, POW, or firebug, the uninvited guest who had made that shadow would have the lodge to himself awhile longer.

She went to get the bike. She couldn't leave Simon and Bobby waiting on the road for the adventure they were counting on. The best they could hope for now was that whoever was inside the lodge would still be there when this fire emergency was over.

16 Meg's mother called at suppertime with good news. A wind shift had turned the Croyden fire away from threatened homes and toward woodland that had been wet down until the water supply failed.

Meg could tell from Gran's side of the conversation that other people on the party line had picked up their telephones and were asking Mom questions at the same time. When Meg and Paul finally got a chance to speak with Mom, there wasn't much time left for them. Mom explained that from now on the lines had to be kept open for essential calls.

The evening news report confirmed what Mom had said. In spite of the many firefighters on hand from New Hampshire and Massachusetts, attempts at holding fire lines were hampered by the shortage of water and pumpers and the lack of two-way radio systems.

"When will the fire be here?" Paul asked.

"It might never come," Gran declared. "Right now it seems to be moving away from us."

Paul scowled. "Still, I'm not going to bed tonight."

"Of course you are. If a fire comes near here, we'll have plenty of warning. You should be rested in case we have to move fast later on."

Paul set his face stubbornly. Meg guessed he would fight off sleep as long as he could. She minded the way the grownups assumed he couldn't take in all the grim talk on the radio. It was the way Aunt Helen and Uncle Frank usually acted with Orin, as if they never expected him to understand.

The radio talk continued to pour out. Hundreds of thousands of board feet of young pine had been destroyed near Kennebunkport, not to mention all the cords of wood, already cut and stacked, that had also gone up in flames. An expert came on and explained that during this postwar building boom timbering operations had left areas of slash—sawdust, chips, and brush where the wood had been cut. The ground fires that started in the slash and spread through scrub oak and berry bushes were even more subject to wind shifts than forest fires.

Mom had told Gran and Ida Kresky and other neighbors on the party line that a call was out for food for the firefighters. So after supper Gran and Aunt Helen went to work making pies and sandwiches. Meg and Paul helped. Paul spread butter and mayonnaise on all the bread in the house. Meg peeled and cored apples.

The radio played music for a while and then issued updates

on the ten fires up north in Aroostook County and the dump fire out toward Norridgewock and the big burn on Mount Desert Island. Meg made a point of telling Paul that all those places were far from Charity Corners, farther even than Portland and Augusta, which were much, much farther than Coventry, where they sometimes went on special occasions.

Gran listened to Meg's efforts and then pitched in with her own. "Come look," she told Paul, shoving aside a ball of pie dough and sprinkling flour on the board. She drew a map with her finger. Here they were, right near Charity Corners, which was in the town of Prescott Falls. Orin was over there, some twelve or so miles to the northwest, this side of Croyden. Mom was off in the other direction, right in the middle of town. Dad was east of Prescott Falls, somewhere near Coventry. Gran made a few other smudges to show Paul other nearby towns like Marks Mills to the west and Lerwick to the south. "Now if I was to include Aroostook County or Mount Desert," she went on, "I'd have to sift my flour over by the cellar stairs or in the bathtub to fit those places on this map. That's how far away from us they are."

Paul laughed. Gran looked pleased. But she was careful to add that there was still a real fire danger close by. No one was forgetting that.

By the time Meg and Paul were sent to bed, the first four pies were cooling on the drainboard, and the next four were in the oven. Tin platters had come out from beneath house plants, and Zac's food dish had been scrubbed and put to use as a makeshift pie tin. Gran gave Paul a bit of overworked dough for the house flowers, but they were already roosting for the night and grumpy at being disturbed. Grace or Disgrace pecked Paul's hand when he opened the cage and reached inside, so he just dropped the pie dough onto the bedding.

After Meg used the privy, she waited for Paul to take his turn there. Then they hurried through the dark back house into the little house, which seemed to be lit from the outside by an eerie yellow glow. They paused a moment to stare out the window but saw only their own faces, both unwashed.

They overslept. But it didn't matter, because Aunt Helen was going to drive the loaded truck into Prescott Falls to take the sandwiches and pies to the canteen that had been set up in the Grange Hall. She could drop off Meg and Paul at school on the way.

They begged to go with her into town so that they could see their mother. Since they were already late, what difference did it make?

"Besides," Meg argued, "nothing much is happening in school. Most of the kids aren't there."

"Your mother's busy," Aunt Helen said.

So another day in school began. Only Mrs. Boudreau was there, though. Miss Wylie, who had been a Red Cross worker during the war, had gone over to Route 1, where a fire had jumped the highway and spread along a ten-mile front. While Miss Wylie was giving first aid to firefighters, her five remaining students were moved into Mrs. Boudreau's room.

"You'll see," Mrs. Boudreau insisted brightly as the children listened in skeptical silence, "everyone's helping. All that big machinery for building the new turnpike is being used to put out fires. The National Guard is setting up roadblocks so the equipment can get through to where it's needed."

But when the children failed to rally to these hopeful signs of progress, she told them she would read to them if she could think of a book the youngest could understand and the oldest would enjoy.

"*Caddie Woodlawn!*" shouted Joyce. Mrs. Boudreau thought that might be over the heads of the first graders. But when Meg pointed out that Paul was the only first grader in school today and he already knew most of the story, Mrs. Boudreau sent Joyce to get the book from the shelf.

Usually Mrs. Boudreau read aloud only when it was too cold and wet for the children to go out at recess. So it felt strange now in the hot, stuffy room with the daylight dimmed outside. The children sat quietly, letting the story carry them far from Maine, where more than forty fires burned. Even when Mrs. Boudreau read the part about the prairie fire that threatened the frontier schoolhouse, it seemed unconnected to the smoke that thickened the air they breathed in this school, in this time.

Mrs. Boudreau picked out one chapter here and one chapter there until, toward the end of the book, she came to the episode in which Caddie's brother mixed up a verse he had to recite in school. Instead of saying, "If at first you don't succeed, try, try again," he was so nervous that out came the silly version "If at first you don't fricassee, fry, fry a hen." Everyone listening to the story laughed at this blunder except Paul, who sat stricken, his face drawn, his mouth agape. He stumbled to his feet. When Mrs. Boudreau asked him if he needed to go to the bathroom, he couldn't reply, couldn't utter a word.

Meg asked if she could take Paul outside for a moment. Mrs. Boudreau nodded. She actually thanked Meg, who couldn't help thinking, as she tugged Paul with her to the door, that if everything were normal and all right, Mrs. Boudreau would probably have told her to mind her own business.

17 They didn't speak until they were sitting on the top step in front of the door. Then Paul drew a breath and said, "I forgot until she read about frying the hen."

"That's in a story—" Meg began.

Paul shook his head. "It was so mixed up this morning because we were late. The house flowers weren't there. I left the cage open last night."

"Well, they're probably around somewhere," Meg told him.

"What about raccoons?"

"Zac would've barked. You know that."

"But they might go away and end up somewhere else. They might be fried like the hen in the story."

"No hen was fried," Meg tried to explain. But that wasn't the point. "I bet the house flowers are home this very minute."

"I never forgot them before," Paul mumbled.

They sat without speaking, inhaling particles of dust and debris stirred by a fitful breeze. It was almost like a storm brewing, except that it was so hot and dry. Meg's eyes and throat stung. Paul wiped his nose on his sleeve.

They could see what looked like a cloud filling the road and rolling toward Charity Corners. Out of the cloud a dog emerged, only to be called away. The cloud grew dense and huge; it drummed on the road and rumbled and smelled of smoke.

"That dog looked like Zac," Paul exclaimed.

Meg stood and peered into the dust cloud. "Cows," she declared. "Our cows?"

They appeared now, lumbering, some of them coughing, all of them with distended nostrils and open mouths. Zac ran from one side to the other to keep them on the straightaway. Uncle Frank, with a stick to tap the road or the hind end of a cow, brought up the rear.

"Uncle Frank," Paul shouted, "did you see Grace and Disgrace?"

Uncle Frank turned their way. "Why aren't you two in school?"

"We are," Meg answered. "We just came out for a minute because Paul's worried about the house flowers."

"Did you see them?" Paul asked again.

"Can't say," Uncle Frank told him. "I've other things on my mind. I'm taking the cows to Lerwick if I can get through."

"All that way?" Meg exclaimed.

"It's not much more than ten or twelve miles. Orin's home. He's helping Helen get Ma out of the house. She thinks she should stay and fight the fire." He shouted to Zac to gather the cows that had wandered into the schoolyard.

"Is Dad home, too?" Meg asked.

Uncle Frank shook his head. "He's staying on in case the wind shifts again. You two will go with Helen and Ma."

Two trucks and a car, all loaded with household valuables, pulled up behind the milling cattle. Zac had to run at the cows' heads to turn them in the right direction. Uncle Frank waved the trucks and car on around him. One truck stayed back. Mr. and Mrs. Leblanc were in it.

"We let the pigs go," Joyce's father told Uncle Frank. "We couldn't think what to do with them. They're on their own now." He paused. "The dog took off after them. He's gone. We called and waited as long as we could."

"He'll make it," Uncle Frank said. "He'll find some place."

The two men looked at each other without saying another word. Finally Mr. Leblanc spoke up. "We're just stopping here for Joyce, so you go on with the cows."

They wished each other luck as they parted. The herd surged forward down the road.

Mrs. Leblanc stepped down from the cab and went into the school. Another car drove up from the opposite direction, waited for the cows to stream around it, and stopped in front of the school. Mrs. Burrows got out just as Joyce and her mother came through the door, followed by Mrs. Boudreau and the remaining children.

Joan Barter sidled up to Paul and sweetly asked whether he had wet his pants. Meg would have hauled off right there in front of everyone if Cindy hadn't stepped in and pulled Joan aside. Cindy's stern look was enough for Meg. She let the insult pass without even bothering to glare at Joan.

Meanwhile the grown-ups were considering the latest information on the fire and trying to decide whether Mrs. Boudreau should send the children home or take them to Marks Mills or Lerwick. Mrs. Leblanc said it was no use trying to call anyone, since all the telephone lines were busy, so they had to work out a plan by themselves. They settled on the Leblancs taking Skip and Nathan and Mrs. Burrows taking the Barter sisters along with Bobby. Mrs. Boudreau would deliver the remaining five children to their homes. Everyone agreed that if there was no vehicle and driver at a child's house, the child would stay with the grown-up in charge.

Mrs. Boudreau went back inside to write a message to be tacked on the schoolhouse door. She wrote the name of each child, the person he or she was with, and the time. It was close to noon. Parents already on their way to school would know who had their children. Absolutely no child would be left off at home unless someone was there at that time.

"What about lunch?" asked Simon.

"Eat in the car," Mrs. Boudreau told him.

Another truck came by and slowed. The driver called to a fifth grader, offering a ride. Mrs. Boudreau didn't know what to do. There could be worried parents waiting at home. The driver said the important thing was to get the kid away from the fire danger. Persuaded, Mrs. Boudreau went back to change the information on the school door, and the truck drove off with its additional passenger.

The four remaining kids piled into Mrs. Boudreau's car. They were too excited to think about food. On Chimney Hill Road they had to stop to let another herd of cows pass. Simon shouted to the cattle driver, asking where he was taking the animals. "Out of here," came the answer. "There's supposed to be a livestock trailer to meet me on the highway. If they let it through." The man's dog dashed in to nip at the heels of cows that were trotting along anyway. Some cows kicked out; others broke ranks to turn on the dog. Mrs. Boudreau drove on, the children suddenly quiet, all of them wondering how the man would get his cows to safety with nothing but a dog like that to help him.

At Simon's house Mrs. Boudreau spoke with Mr. Farris, who was hosing down tarps spread over stacked lumber. Debris swirled around him: cinders and leaves and twigs.

"As far as I can make out," Simon's father remarked, "a fire can miss a building next to one it takes. Depends how fast it's traveling and what the wind's up to. So you don't dare leave anything to chance." He pointed to the house, where Simon's mother was hosing the roof.

"Wouldn't it be better to save the water for when the fire's closer?" Simon asked him.

"Son," said Mr. Farris, "when it's closer than this, it'll be too close for comfort. Go help your mother."

At Meg's house Mrs. Boudreau didn't have to go up the driveway or speak to anyone, because both Aunt Helen and Gran were in plain sight. So were the truck and, just behind it, Toby and June hitched to the wagon.

But after Mrs. Boudreau had dropped off Meg and Paul and driven on, the children hung back because Aunt Helen was hollering at Gran in a voice that was shrill with desperation.

"We have to get going," Aunt Helen screeched.

"Not without Orin," Gran shouted back as she marched briskly over the hill beyond the house.

"He's coming. He knows what to do, where to go," Aunt Helen shrilled. She ran after Gran. Now Meg could hear her yelling at Orin somewhere down the sloping field that Meg's father had plowed only a few days before. "You finish up now. The horses are fussing. Orin, you hear me?"

Meg couldn't hear or see over the crest of the hill, but she figured Orin must have called back a reply that seemed to satisfy Gran as well as Aunt Helen, because the shouting ceased. Meg started toward the house; she meant to wait for them beside the truck. But Paul dashed past her and on through the door.

Meg followed to bring him out. She found him in the dim back house beyond the empty, open cage. He was scuttling around barrels and boxes, frantically hunting for his hens.

By the time she managed to yank him outside, the truck was chugging down the driveway to the road. Meg raced after it, screaming at the top of her lungs. But the wind was screaming, too, and burnt stuff blew inside her mouth, choking her.

Anyway, Aunt Helen and Gran were at each other again, so they couldn't hear a thing Meg yelled.

18 Mrs. Boudreau had clearly written on the notice that no children would be left on their own. But that was exactly what Meg and Paul now were. Aunt Helen and Gran would stop, read the notice on the school door, and drive on, believing the children safe with Mrs. Boudreau.

Meg was trying to digest all this when Paul came up behind her and said, "I can't find the house flowers."

"They've taken the truck," Meg replied, turning to face him. "They've gone without us."

"The house flowers? Grace and Disgrace?"

"Oh, Paul, no. I'm talking about Gran and Aunt Helen. We've been left behind."

"Good," Paul said. "I have time to look for them before the wagon goes."

They both looked at Toby and June, who were stamping and tossing their heads and shaking their reins.

"Who's going to drive them?" Paul asked.

Meg shook her head. Then she ran to the upper edge of the plowed field, cupped her hands to her mouth, and shouted down the hill to Orin, who was walking along the lower border of the field tipping water out of a milk can. What made him think he could pour enough to stop a fire?

She waited for him to work his way closer. If he turned uphill toward the house, then maybe he would hear her. Only now a plane droned overhead. It circled so low that Meg could see the pilot, who leaned out over the side with a megaphone.

"Fire's nearly here," he boomed through the megaphone. "You've got twenty minutes or so. Better get out now."

Orin straightened up from his dousing. He pointed toward the woods.

"That's right," the pilot shouted. "Wind changed again."

Orin waved at him and went back to wetting down the dry grass and brush that edged the plowed earth.

Paul yelled up at the pilot, "Did you see two black hens?" But the plane was rising into the charcoal sky. Its droning engine could be heard moments after it had disappeared from view. Then it was gone altogether.

Turning the corner, Orin started uphill. But he must have used up all the water because he held the milk can upside down and shook it. Then he ran up toward the house. When he caught sight of Meg and Paul, he registered no surprise. He just raced past them.

"Orin!" Meg shouted. "You heard that man in the plane. Let's go now. Look how jumpy the horses are."

Pausing, Orin glanced at Toby and June. Then he pointed

to the sodden blankets draped along the foundation of the house. "Get them over the horses," he told her. "Onto them."

Paul said, "Orin, did you see Grace and Disgrace?"

Orin shook his head. He said they would leave as soon as he finished. He dashed into the house.

"Help me," Meg ordered as she tugged a blanket away from the foundation. But Paul was too frantic to respond. The blanket was so heavy with water she had to drag it to the horses. She struggled to lift it up over Toby's withers, but he towered over her. Anyway, what was the point? Even if she could get it onto him, wouldn't it slide off as soon as the horses started to pull the wagon?

She glanced back at the house. Orin was coming out with the kerosene tank from the stove. He must have filled it with water, too.

Running to meet him, Paul waved his hands as if trying to describe something. Meg turned back to the horses. Grasping one corner of the blanket, she managed to climb from pole to harness. Toby started when she dragged the cold, wet blanket over his rump. She had to straddle him backward as she hauled the blanket along his back. She kept talking to him to calm him, telling him they would be all right. Telling herself, too.

She was on her way back for another blanket when she heard a clanging below the house. Paul was dragging the empty milk can and banging it with a stick.

She had a better idea how to handle the second blanket and almost had it over June's back when she heard Paul shout. One black hen was flapping toward him. The other emerged from the barn loft door, hurtled down, and half flew above the plowed section that separated the house from the barn. Peeping and squawking as if it couldn't decide whether it was a chick or a hen, it tumbled toward Paul.

"It worked," Paul yelled down to Orin. He clutched both

hens so tightly that their feathers stuck out through his fingers.

"Don't let go," Meg told him, jumping to the ground and starting for the barn. "I'll find something to put them in." But what she saw on her way downhill brought her up short. Orin was near the tongue of woodland that met the plowed field at the farthest corner. She screamed at him because he didn't seem to see the bank of smoke pushing through the trees.

The plane was back, circling. She could hear the pilot boom through the megaphone: "You can't make Charity Corners. Go the other way. You hear me?"

Orin waved, but as the plane gained altitude, he appeared to ignore the warning. He stooped, then sprang back and darted along the edge of the field, only to stoop farther on. Flames shot up where he had stopped.

"Orin!" Meg screamed.

He paid no attention. Probably he couldn't hear her. Racing to the barn, she groped in the feed room for a burlap bag. As she ran outside with the bag, she cast an eye downhill. Orin was turning the corner now, approaching Paul and shouting at him to get on the wagon. Still, Orin stopped once more, striking a match, setting fire to the edge of the field.

As she clutched the burlap bag with clammy hands and watched the line of flames spread and scud over the grassland toward the woods, it finally came to her that Orin had been dribbling kerosene, not water, along the downhill border and partway up toward the house. She couldn't stop staring as the fire reached the trees, dancing wildly like a spirit released from captivity. It was Paul who called her out of her trance, Paul needing the bag for the hens.

By the time she reached the wagon, Orin was there, too, whipping the blankets off the horses. "What are you doing?" she shrieked at him.

"They're wet enough," he told her as he spread the blankets

over the wagonload and ordered her and Paul to climb underneath. He boosted Paul up, then handed him the bagged hens.

"No," Paul protested. "I want to see."

Meg objected, too. She wasn't about to let Orin drive off without keeping an eye on him. Not after what she had just seen. "We can crawl underneath if we have to," she declared. "Not now."

So they knelt side by side, next to Orin, who shook the reins and clucked to the horses, heading out. Not to Charity Corners.

19 Orin turned the horses to the right. They lurched forward, out of step with each other, tossing their heads and snorting.

Orin told Paul to set down the burlap bag and hold on to the wagon with both hands.

"The hens might get out," Paul objected. "They might fall off."

Orin handed the reins to Meg. Twisting the top of the bag into a knot, he wedged it between a pile of winter coats and a sack of oats. The hens had given in to the darkness inside the bag; they didn't make a sound.

"Can they breathe like that?" Meg asked.

Orin nodded. "Better than us when the smoke comes."

She stared at his smudged and blistered face. Aunt Helen must have made him change, because his clothes weren't burned at all. Champ's jacket was tied around his waist, the sleeves pulled through Orin's belt.

Meg couldn't read his expression. Not that it ever registered much, except in the old days when Champ would dare Orin to join him in some reckless feat and then make a joke of it, whatever the outcome. It was a long time since Meg had seen Orin's slow smile, his face lighting up. She had always assumed it was Champ's attention that made Orin happy. But maybe it was something else. Maybe it was the thrill of danger. Is that why he had delayed their escape to start a fire of his own? Did he suppose it made no difference since the big fire was coming anyway?

But after days on the fireline in Croyden, wouldn't even Orin have had enough of danger?

As he urged the horses on, he kept glancing to the right across the ridge, where swirling leaves and twigs and other debris formed airborne whirlpools.

Meg couldn't shake the notion that a storm was about to break. Any minute now there might be a downpour, right here, right on top of them, putting out the fire wherever it was. Then they could go home.

Only the wind was hot, hotter than anything she had ever felt before.

Paul said, "I forgot my lunch. I'm hungry."

Meg, who had tossed hers up on the wagon, crawled back to get it. She gave half her sandwich to Paul and offered the other half to Orin, who said he had already eaten plenty. So she ate it herself and gave her apple to Paul.

"I have to pee," he announced when all the food was gone.

Orin handed the reins over to Meg again and steadied Paul as he knelt on a mattress. The horses slowed.

"Git up!" Orin shouted at them. Taking over from Meg, he slapped their rumps with the ends of the reins. The horses broke into a gallop. As far as Meg knew, this was the first time they had ever galloped in harness. Maybe a storm was coming after all. She had seen them gallop before thunder and lightning.

She looked skyward, only to find that there was no sky. Darkness had closed over them. Even below, where the woods receded, the open land admitted no light. Here was the Kresky place, the house so diminished by the swirling darkness that it looked unreal, like a doll's house.

"I hear a train," Paul said. "I didn't know there was a train here."

"We're almost at the bridge," Meg told him. But the roaring didn't come from up ahead. It came from the woods behind the Kresky house.

"Git up!" Orin yelled at Toby and June.

"Look!" cried Paul, pointing toward a deer that bounded toward them. It crossed the road in front of the horses, switched directions, and raced ahead of them.

Meg saw other animals scurrying out from the blackness behind the Kresky house. It was almost as if the train had jumped its tracks and were chasing them all onto the road.

At the fork Orin had to slow the horses to make the left turn downhill. Meg grabbed Paul as he rocked first one way and then another. She glanced back at the fleeing animals just in time to catch a glimpse of an enormous orange balloon bouncing from treetop to treetop. The trees seemed to be playing ball with it, tossing it back and forth. Then in an instant the balloon burst, and a solid wall of fire dropped like a giant curtain from the trees. Everything danced and seethed. Only the Kresky house stood firm and solid before the wall of flame. Then it exploded. It looked something like a newsreel picture of a bombing. One moment the house was there, and the next it was blown apart.

The horses careered down the hill, Orin yelling and flailing at them. Something shaken loose fell to the road with a clatter. Meg was bounced so hard now that she didn't dare lean out to see what it was they had lost.

Where the road leveled off, Orin reined in the horses again. He gazed all around like an animal testing the wind, the air, the danger. Then he whipped the horses forward through thick smoke. Even though they coughed and gasped, he forced them on.

The scorching wind battered them with sticks and pine-cones and clusters of acorns and even clumps of dry moss torn from the forest floor. Something landed beside the road and set dead leaves ablaze. The horses galloped faster.

Orin shouted at Meg and Paul to get under one of the soaked blankets. But when they tried to pull it over them, they were nearly flung off. So they stayed at the front of the wagon, clinging to a crossboard that rattled and shook.

Meg kept stealing glances at the load. When an ember landed on the mattress, she screamed at Orin to look. After handing her the reins once more, he had to detach his leg from Paul's clutches before he could scramble back. Meg was terrified that Orin would lose his balance while he tried to smother the burning mattress with a wet blanket. But some-thing else caught fire, something wrapped in paper, and so he ended up dumping the mattress and the parcel on the road behind them.

He got back to driving just before the sharp curve where the road crossed the railroad tracks. Instead of slowing for the bumpy crossing, he took the tracks at breakneck speed, dumping more cargo no longer packed in by the mattress.

Meg couldn't think anymore. There was nothing but heat and wind and tiny flying flames and the terrible rattling and roaring. She knew they would have to cross the tracks once more. Soon. This time they would probably get shaken off, all three of them. She wasn't able to think beyond the hurtling wagon. All she knew was that it would be a relief to stand on the unmoving ground.

Nothing made sense now. Not Orin setting fire to their own home. Nor his driving the horses all the way around to the far end of Alder Swamp Road, as if he knew exactly where he was heading. Driving his beloved Toby and June and his two younger cousins back toward the fire.

But at the bridge Orin hauled in and stopped the horses. Jumping from the wagon, he shouted to Meg and Paul to follow. But Meg was still holding on for dear life. Dazed, she couldn't let go.

Paul whimpered, "I want to stay here."

Reaching up, Orin yanked him off the wagon.

"Grace!" Paul wailed. "Disgrace."

"Loose the horses," Orin told Meg. Climbing up to get the burlap bag, he shoved her sideways. "Loose them."

Slowly, unsteadily, Meg slid to the road. The ground wasn't as firm as she had expected. It seemed to shift and roll under her. She grabbed Toby's singletree for support and started to unbuckle his trace-bearer.

Behind her Orin said, "Never mind all that. Just unhitch them."

But the horses strained forward, leaving no slack for Meg to unhook them.

Orin called to her from June's side. "Take Paul. Under the bridge."

She grabbed Paul's hand. He dropped the bag, crying out. She snatched it up and dragged him to where the bank plummeted to the stream, now dry. There was a culvert, half buried in soil and stones. Leaning down to look in, she recoiled from the sour stench inside.

Stones tumbled down and clattered beside her and Paul. Orin appeared, dragging June, the wet blanket over her head and neck. She resisted him, bearing back, almost sitting on her hindquarters.

Meg hauled herself up by roots and stumps until she was in back of June. Grabbing a stick, she swatted at her rump.

70

June stiffened, then leaped clumsily forward, landing on her knees.

Orin gave June enough rein to allow her to stagger to her feet. Then he straightened the blanket and tied her to a reinforcing rod that protruded from the concrete side of the underbridge. Without a word he struggled back up the embankment. Meg thought he had gone for Toby, but he returned without him.

"Where's Toby?" Meg cried.

"Gone," Orin said, thrusting Paul and the sack inside the culvert. "Get in there," he told Meg.

"Gone where?" she asked. "What will happen to him?"

"Probably he'll come. He always stays with June. Get in."

Scooching down, she crawled on her hands and knees. Orin was right behind her. She could feel him trembling.

"It stinks here," Paul said. "How long do we have to stay?"

Meg told him to hush.

"Is the fire coming?"

She gave Orin time to reply, and when he didn't, she said, "No. Not here."

Paul subsided. Turning sideways, he backed against the incurving wall of the culvert, then stuck his legs straight out. He dragged the burlap bag onto his lap and began to open it.

"Keep that closed," Orin ordered. "If those chickens get away, no one's going after them."

"Why not?" Paul retorted. "I will. Anyway, you can't boss me."

Orin spoke to Meg. "I'm going to check June."

"Can I come, too?" asked Paul.

"No," Orin shouted as he crawled out. Meg guessed he wanted to see whether Toby had shown up.

"Orin's mean," Paul grumbled. "He never used to be."

Meg couldn't think of anything to say.

Paul raised grubby fists to his eyes. "I want a grown-up," he whimpered. "I don't want to be here."

Rearranging herself onto her knees, Meg put her arm around Paul. But still no words of comfort came to her. She wanted a grown-up, too.

Orin came diving back inside. He was panting like Zac after a hard chase. He huddled beside Meg, and then the whole world lurched and the culvert shook. So did everything in it. The roaring they had heard before bore down on them.

"A train!" cried Paul. "It's coming. It'll run over us."

He darted toward the opening on his side, found it mostly blocked, and hurled himself across Meg. Orin caught him, held him.

"It's not a train," Orin shouted through the roaring. "Tell him," Orin yelled at Meg.

But Meg recognized this din. Nothing else she knew of could overwhelm every other sound like this but a steam-driven freight train with its hammering pistons and its clacking wheels. It was so close now that she couldn't hear another thing Orin shouted.

Paul, struggling to break free, kicked at Orin, flailed out, and hit her instead. She ignored this pummeling. She just cowered, head down, instinctively adopting the position they used to practice in school for air-raid drills.

The train roared over as if it meant to bury them. In its headlong rush, with its terrible force, it must have knocked loose all kinds of stones, because things pinged and banged and clattered long after it had charged by.

20 Despite the searing heat, Meg did not stir. She seemed to be waiting for something. Maybe she needed to hear Mrs. Boudreau's all-clear before raising her head from her knees. She felt Paul's utter stillness, Orin's.

Her eyes were streaming tears. When she rubbed them and finally opened them, everything was blurred. Yet there was more light inside the culvert. Orin had his head back, his eyes still closed. Paul lay facedown across Orin's knees. He looked asleep.

Turning to check on the hens, Meg thought they must have escaped from the burlap bag, because what looked at first like one of them was huddled beside the bag. She rubbed her eyes some more to clear her vision and realized that she was staring at a bedraggled crow, not a black bantam hen.

The crow was not alone. Meg caught sight of a skunk and then a mouse and two squirrels. This unlikely assortment of animals, all immobile, was clustered at the nearly blocked end of the culvert. She kept rubbing her eyes and peering at the animals. They eyed her, too. But only when she extended a hand toward them did they break from their trancelike stillness and shrink from her. They might have escaped through the clogged end of the culvert, but not one of them tried to get away. Then all at once she realized that one other animal was there at the end. It was larger than the others, with a blunt face and piercing eyes. Too sleek to be a beaver, she guessed. An otter? A weasel?

As she grew used to her tearing eyes, she began to make out more mice and at least three rabbits bunched together. None of them seemed to take any notice of the larger animal, which also ignored them. Every single creature looked stuck, not because it couldn't escape from the culvert but because each one of them was somehow sealed within this moment, as if time had stopped.

Paul drew his legs under him. Gulping, he moaned a little and then slid from Orin's knees. "Meg?" He was whispering, as if he had just awakened.

"Yes," she answered softly.

"The train ran over us for a long time. It was awful."

"Ssh," she said. "Be very quiet. I want to show you something."

Without seeming to move a muscle, Orin spoke in his ordinary tone. "That wasn't a train. That was fire."

"You're teasing," Paul said.

"It sounded like one of those long, long freight trains," Meg told Paul as she tried to turn him toward the animals. But they weren't there anymore, not one of them. And because her eyes were so teary and she felt so strange and muddled, she wondered whether she had dreamed them up.

Yet their presence lingered. At the edge of the smell of burning an unmistakable reek of wild fur and feathers still clung to the stale, hot air inside the culvert.

"What?" demanded Paul.

"June!" blurted Orin, lurching forward. He scrambled out his end.

Paul started after him. Meg grabbed at Paul. There was no telling what Orin would find. "Wait," she ordered.

They breathed together, tasting smoke and the acrid scent of the creatures that had shared this cramped space with them. While they sat there, Mrs. Boudreau's instruction for surviving smoke and fire came to Meg. Orin must have known exactly what he was doing when he brought them down here to the lowest possible level. Orin knew. And so had the wild animals.

Where were they now? Would they be safe aboveground?

Orin stuck his head inside to report that June had some burns but was all right. He told Meg and Paul they could come out, but on their feet because the ground was still so hot.

Meg nudged Paul along. Now that he was allowed to, he was reluctant to leave the culvert. Orin helped him stand and then picked him up to make room for Meg.

At first Meg doubted what Orin had said about the fire. The stream bed looked the same. There was June, still tied, the blanket draped over her. Maybe there was a little more rubble lying about. That was all.

But as soon as Meg stepped away from beneath the bridge and peered up the embankment, she saw coils of smoke rising from blackened stumps of trees.

"Let's go home now," Paul pleaded.

"No," Orin told him. "I'm going to the road."

"Me, too," Paul declared.

Orin carried him. Meg stayed beside June, listening to her painful, rasping breaths.

"Meg, you," Orin called down to her. "Come. Keep Paul."

It was tough climbing. When Meg grabbed a root to pull herself up, it burned her hand. She cried out. Maybe Orin would rush to help her the way a grown-up might. But this was Orin, not Dad or Uncle Frank.

"Come on," he drawled, his voice tinged with impatience. "I still have to get June."

He was different with the horse, crooning to her and giving her time to find the right footholds in the steep, crumbling slope. But her hoofs dug too deeply, carving craters that made the bank cave in. She kept coughing as she floundered. Each time she had to stop, he gave her a moment to quiet down before coaxing her once more up the treacherous bank.

"It's burned," he said to Meg. "Everything in the ground burns, so it can't hold together. It just breaks up."

He was speaking of the soil. But Meg sensed he was saying

something more than that, too. The way he had after Gran had to tell him that Champ had been killed. "They make mistakes," he had declared. "The army. Ask Champ. He says the army's dumber than me." Later Meg had found him slouched astride a sawhorse, Champ's fishing rod across his knee. "Champ said I could use this while he's away," Orin had informed her. "But I might break it, you know. Like I broke mine. So . . ." Orin had paused, sucking in air and letting it seep out in a tuneless whistle. "So I'm saving it for him. Not using it." Then his voice had risen. "I'm scared it'll get broken." She had stood before him in tears, unable to say that Champ was never coming back.

Standing before him now, she longed to ask about Toby but didn't dare. Anyway, what could Orin possibly know? Probably he was thinking, as she was, that not much could have survived the fire that had raged over their heads and had left in its wake this vast, smoking wasteland full of tree skeletons, with hundreds of small flames lapping hungrily at anything that remained.

21

It was hard to walk away from what was left of the wagon and its contents. Hubs and contorted wheel rims still smoked. Little else was recognizable. Even the churn, the glass one that Gran really used to make butter, had melted down, the twisted crank lodged in some misshapen mass.

Orin seemed aimless now, as if he had spent all his energy saving them from the onrushing fire and could deal with nothing more. He stood at June's head, his arms slightly extended but somehow useless.

In the distance a rabbit emerged from a burrow. It raised

itself on its haunches to stare all around. Meg could feel its bewilderment. The fire had made them equal, each unable to absorb what had become of the known landscape.

She started to wonder about Toby again, then quickly shoved the thought of him aside.

She listened to June squeaking with every breath she drew. June's ears flicked forward as she caught sight of the rabbit. The rabbit, its nose twitching, stared at June for an instant and then raced away.

Ash feathers blown on a backdraft floated onto June's broad back and head. Absently Orin brushed them out of her mane and forelock.

Paul said, "I'm thirsty."

No one answered him. From far off a fire whistle hooted. Three blasts, a break, three blasts, another break, and three more blasts. That was the general alarm for Prescott Falls. It was comforting to identify it, to call up ordinary, recognizable landmarks like the post office and Grange and town hall, the mill and the hardware store, Libby's Market and the war memorial on the green with Champ's name on it, and the bridge and the schools across the river. Probably Mom was in town right now. Unless they had evacuated the telephone exchange.

Meg said to Orin, "What should we do?"

He shrugged.

Meg tried again. "You think it's safe to go on Alder Swamp Road?"

"I guess," Orin replied.

"Or should we go back?" she suggested. "Try to go home?"

Orin shook his head. "I was to drive the horses to the pond." But he didn't move.

"Come on, then." Hoisting the burlap bag, she led the way. Paul followed, stopping often to look back at the place in the road where the wagon had stood.

Orin led June, who was painfully slow. "Out of the way," he said to Paul from time to time, as if it were Paul rather than the horse that held Orin back. June plodded listlessly, a machine that had all but run down.

Farther along they came to the black and swollen carcass of a pig. It might have been one of those Mr. Leblanc had let out. Paul circled it once and then scrambled to catch up with Meg, who refused to give it more than a passing glance. He slipped his hand into hers.

"There are two more off the road," he told her.

"Two more what?" Meg said, not wanting to know, not wanting the answer he was bound to give.

"Pigs," said Paul. "Pigs all burned up."

In time they walked out of the heat and into an area less ravaged. Meg began to breathe more easily. A few trees stood fully branched, but with smoke seeping out of them. One suddenly toppled as if wrenched from the ground. When it thudded to the forest floor, the trunk disintegrated before their eyes. They gaped at it. June seemed to drift off to sleep. Orin leaned against her. Meg set off again, feeling the air cool down as she walked. Soon she heard June plodding behind her.

Up ahead the road turned. Meg could see beyond the burn to live trees. She saw a house and barn and machine shed, all startlingly intact. For a while she was able to keep this living scene in view on one side of the road while on the other side stretched seemingly endless reaches of scorched earth.

Then the wasteland appeared again on both sides. It made no sense. How could the fire leave one place unscathed while destroying everything else?

She suggested to Orin that they go back to that house. He shook his head.

"Why not?" she demanded. "They'd have a well there. We could get water."

"No," he mumbled, "not safe."

When she started to argue, he pointed to the tiny pillars of smoke, the fitful flames. "Wind changes, we're trapped."

She felt like asking what made him think they couldn't be trapped where they were heading, but she knew it would be pointless. Once Orin got hold of a notion, he was the stubbornest person alive. "Won't be budged," Uncle Frank would complain about Orin. "Might be different if he knew something."

Gran always spoke up for Orin. "Knows a deal more than you credit," she would tell her son. Once after Meg had come home from school with her dress torn and her knee bloody, Gran had taken her to task for getting into another fight. "It can't make the children like Orin any better," Gran had pointed out. "Besides, it won't be easy to mend your frock, and new clothes don't grow on trees."

Meg had replied that the kids didn't have to like Orin; they just had to leave him alone. Suddenly bold, she had added, "I bet you would've done it."

"Me?" Gran had exclaimed. "Me in a schoolyard brawl?"

And they had burst out laughing at the thought, the scolding over, the point taken.

The afternoon seemed endless. After a while Meg realized that she had stopped looking at anything but the road directly in front of her. As she trudged on, she became aware that Paul was hanging back. Every once in a while he whimpered, but he didn't utter a word. He had stopped asking for a rest, for water, for food, for Mom. He looked as though he had stopped believing in them at all.

Meg broke the long silence. Turning to Orin, she asked if he could put Paul on June's back.

Orin couldn't muster a reply. He simply nodded and picked Paul up. But when Paul felt the clammy blanket under him, he squirmed and tried to draw his legs up under him.

"We could leave that blanket here," Meg suggested. "We could get it later when there's a car."

Orin shook his head.

"Why not?" Meg insisted. "Orin, you're not in charge of everything."

Rolling the blanket away from Paul, Orin heaved it over his shoulder. He didn't even bother to respond to Meg with a look. That was his usual way. He seldom met her eye, or anyone else's, for that matter. Meg had long guessed that it was this kind of disregard that had spared him whenever the kids at school taunted him. He would become absent, leaving Meg to smart and fume at the names they called or the tricks they played on him. Meg had never understood his remoteness; she didn't understand it now.

On they went, Paul leaning over the horse collar and clasping the brass hames, his cheek resting on June's mane. Meg shifted the bag with the hens from one hand to the other. Even though they weighed practically nothing, the bag kept her off-balance. Inside her head she thought a song and tried to march to its rhythm. "You put your right foot in, you put your right foot out. . . ." Only she wasn't following its directions. She was just stepping left and right and left and right, her eyes nearly shut because they stung so.

The bag swung back and forth, sometimes whacking against her leg and prompting a small squawk from inside. She blocked out that sound. She concentrated on moving forward, comforted by the good horse smell that sometimes came to her in spite of the fire stench inside her nostrils.

22 All at once Meg's nose informed her that they had entered living woods. Suddenly there wasn't only the horse smell to counter the reek of charred wood. There was the sweet and pungent aroma of balsam fir. Meg opened her eyes. June pressed ahead in a sudden eager surge. Orin, who had dropped the reins, staggered behind.

"What's happened?" Meg asked him. "What's got her going?"

"Water," he said.

Still, it took time for Meg to recognize this stretch of road. They were approaching Charity Pond from the Croyden road. She wanted to whoop and cheer and run, but she was afraid Paul might fall off June. So she just scrambled to catch up and grabbed the dragging reins.

As soon as June left the road and crossed the trail between Miss Trilling's lodge and the three cabins on the north shore, Meg felt like flinging herself to the ground to touch her own footsteps, to find the self she had lost today, the girl who had helped invent a spy so that she and her friends could prove themselves heroes.

When branches began to whack at Paul, Orin helped him down. Then Orin looped the long reins up through June's collar and gave her a slap of dismissal. She crashed through the dry trees and undergrowth, branches snapping, hoofs striking stones. Then came splashings.

Meg and Paul tore along the path that June's huge bulk had broken for them. They didn't stop to take off clothes, although Meg did pause to deposit the burlap bag on the mossy bank. Then she ran after Paul until the water slowed her. Sinking to her knees, she dipped her face into the cool shallows, already silted by the horse that wallowed farther out.

"Stupid," Orin pronounced as he untied the sleeves of his brother's jacket and removed his grandfather's boots. He shed his pants and shirt before wading into the pond. "You won't have anything dry to put on," he told Meg and Paul.

They didn't care. Not now, while the water slid over their hot, aching bodies and cradled them with gentle buoyancy. Nothing existed for them but this delicious feeling.

June was the first to leave the pond, Orin quick to follow and catch her. He tied her to the slender trunk of a black ash and then called his cousins out of the pond. "It'll be dark soon," he said.

Meg looked around. How could Orin tell? They had come through the longest darkness of their lives. Some of it had even invaded this pond, for a gray pall screened out the sun so that only an orange blur was reflected on the metallic surface of the water. This was all that Orin had to go by. Yet he knew that night was coming just as he had known to send them into the lowest possible place while the fire stormed over them.

She drew Paul with her out of the pond and was instantly cold. Paul clutched himself, shivering convulsively. Their dripping clothes seemed to bind them in a sudden autumn chill.

For one foolish second Meg thought of making a fire in one of the outdoor fireplaces. The notion just slipped into her mind because it was what you did when you were freezing and wet. She actually started to wonder where she could find matches. That brought her to Orin. She saw him again, saw him bobbing along the border of the plowed field while flames shot up behind him. How could she imagine starting a fire?

She shivered, too, although whether from being chilled or from the sheer horror of that recollection, she couldn't tell.

Orin removed Paul's drenched shirt and wrapped him in Champ's jacket. Then Orin tugged June along her trodden path to the trail. Meg saw that he was heading for Miss Trilling's. She picked up the burlap bag. Grace, or Disgrace, squawked and then muttered a bit. Meg looked at Paul, whose lips and fingers had turned blue. She jiggled the bag, hoping to produce two hen complaints, then gave up. She hoped she wouldn't find one of the hens dead when the bag was finally opened.

By the time Meg and Paul reached the stable, Orin had the harness off June and was just turning her into the little paddock. After that he walked all around the stable and carriage house.

Meg guessed he was looking for a way in. She knew from hay deliveries with her father that the big sliding door was hooked inside. She also knew where to find the key to the walk-in door. She nearly told Orin. She had to check that impulse. This was no time to give away secrets to a backward boy who set fires.

Waiting until Orin had started around again, she reached behind the upturned water trough where the board-and-batten wall overlapped the stone foundation. Her groping fingers made contact with the key that hung there on a nail.

Quickly she ran to the walk-in door on the side nearest the lodge. She managed to get the door open before Orin reappeared.

"Here!" she shouted to Paul, to Orin, calling them in as she might have called Zac to the house. Paul had been in the carriage house before, but she doubted that Orin had ever seen anything this neat and elegant.

Pointing to the loft stairs, she told him it would be all right to borrow some hay for June. Anyway, she thought to herself, Miss Trilling wasn't likely to notice that some was taken. Still, Meg would have to make sure that Orin didn't get blamed for helping himself to that hay.

This was always the threat Champ had used to keep Meg from telling on him. "You know who'll get blamed," Champ would warn. "If you don't watch your step, Orin'll be in a heap of trouble." Knowing that as far as Uncle Frank was concerned Champ could do no wrong, while Orin could seldom do anything right, Meg had learned to keep her mouth shut.

This time, though, it wasn't Uncle Frank she needed to worry about but Dad, who was so proper about everything to do with the lodge. Sometimes Gran would cast a scornful glance his way and remind him that Miss Trilling wasn't royalty. But Dad had been raised to look up to the Trillings. This arrangement had worked for his father and for him, and he intended it to go on working for his children as well.

Meg showed Orin up the stairs to the loft and switched on the light for him. A moment later he descended with his arms full of hay, which he carried out the door and around to June. Meg didn't show him the way through the stable; he would only scatter hay on the floor.

Paul opened the burlap bag. The two black hens tumbled out, feathers askew, beaks agape. For a moment they seemed dazed. One of them had an eye swollen shut. She circled dizzily with her head tilted to one side. Then she caught sight of a bug and tottered over to it. The other hen darted in, collided, and then went wild at the sight of fresh prey below the windows. Both hens set to work on the flies, dead and alive, killing them over and over again and clucking with joy.

When Orin returned, he was carrying the damp blanket. Up in the hayloft Meg and Paul took off their wet clothes and huddled together under it. When Paul started to shiver again,

Meg went down to the tack room to look for something dry. Sure enough, two light horse blankets were draped over the saddle racks. Not only that, but there was also a barn jacket and a flannel shirt on one of the hooks. Wearing both of these, Meg dragged the horse blankets up to the loft.

She gave one to Orin and the flannel shirt to Paul. Then she pulled the other horse blanket over Paul and herself. Tense with cold, she tried to recall the searing heat from the fire. But it didn't help to remember. It didn't help to conjure up one extreme to fend off another. Besides, for all she knew, the air wasn't all that different from before. This cold seemed to be lodged inside herself, her bones turned to ice.

After Paul finally went limp beside her, she relaxed enough to find the few warm spots that existed here and there. She tucked her hands under her chin and tried to bury one foot beneath the other. The warmth began to spread a little. With a final shuddering sigh, she gave in to exhaustion and to the close, sheltered darkness of the loft.

23 A droning sound woke them. A spotter plane, they guessed. Yet none of them stirred; none of them wanted to quit the warmth and the peace.

It occurred to Meg that it might be the same pilot who had warned Orin yesterday. Maybe the pilot was looking for them. But even if she ran outside, how would he see her through the trees? She dozed.

Orin and Paul must have drifted off, too, because they all sat up with a start at the blast of a fire whistle coming from a new direction. At least new for them.

"Not Croyden," Orin declared. "I know Croyden."

"It's far away," Meg said. "I think," she added, hoping Orin would agree with her.

He said, "You can't tell. The wind does funny things." Then he thrust off the blanket, grabbed an armful of hay, and went downstairs. Meg heard the house flowers beg for crumbs. She heard him growl at them. Then the door slammed.

By the time she was dressed and outside, Orin was leading June back from the pond. That made her think of water for the hens. She called up to Paul, telling him where to find a bucket in the stable and to give Grace and Disgrace a drink. Then she asked Orin where they were going next.

"Nowhere," he told her. "I'm going. You and Paul stay."

"We can't do that, Orin. We're hungry. They'll be worried. If we go up to the road, someone will give us a ride into town."

Orin shook his head. "We don't know where the fire is. We don't know anything."

"So the fire could come here," she argued. "While you're gone."

"There's the pond. There's June. You're fine."

"I don't want to," she told him. "I don't want to stay here alone."

"You're not alone. You have Paul."

"You know what I mean." Panic seized her. She knew it made no sense to look to Orin for support, but she couldn't keep herself from babbling, "Please, please. Anyway," she blurted, "it's dangerous here. There's a spy hiding out in the lodge."

"Huh?" Orin sent her a look of disbelief.

"Maybe not a spy exactly. An escaped prisoner of war." She could hear how far-fetched that sounded. Without Simon to bolster her, it seemed like pure nonsense.

"Now you're like the other kids," Orin said. "You think you can fool me." He turned on his heel.

Stung, she nearly burst out at him about the fire he had

set. Choking back her anger, she said instead, "I've never fooled you. I never would."

Orin shrugged and stumped up the driveway.

Paul came outside and asked where Orin was.

"Gone," Meg answered bleakly. Then she added, "He'll be back as soon as he finds out where it's safe for us to go."

"Is he going to bring something to eat?"

"Probably. Or anyway someone else will come. In a car."

"If the plane comes back, can we fly away in it?"

Meg shook her head. "There's no place to land around here."

"Does he know we're here?"

Meg gulped. When she told Paul she didn't think so, that no one knew where they were, she had to blink back tears. How long would it take for Mom or Dad to discover that she and Paul weren't with Mrs. Boudreau?

"I'm lonely," Paul said.

"So am I." The words came out a whisper. If only someone would show up, anyone at all, even good Cindy Barter or her rotten sister, Joan. Even a real spy or a prisoner of war.

Paul started toward the lodge.

"Don't go there," she called to him.

"I just want to look at the window pictures," he said.

But what if that crazy notion about someone hiding inside was true after all? "There are pictures in the carriage house," she told him. "Let's look at them first."

There was plenty to keep him busy there, framed photographs of fancy show horses with rosettes on their bridles. In one picture a young woman, beaming with pride, sat astride her perfectly groomed horse.

"I bet that's Miss Trilling," Meg remarked.

Paul laughed. "That's a girl," he declared.

"Miss Trilling long ago," Meg added, suddenly recalling the time Miss Trilling had spoken about summers at the lodge when she was a child. In those days there had been more servants than members of the family. It was hard to believe that Miss Trilling could remember all kinds of details through so many distant years. Then Dad had mentioned that the carriage in one of the framed photographs had still been kept here when he was a boy. Meg had fastened on this memory. Dad would never make that up, so he was like a bridge she could cross in her mind to olden times.

After a while Paul grew bored with the old-fashioned photographs. "Let's go somewhere else," he said.

"The hayloft," she proposed as though it were a new, exciting possibility.

"We were just there," he objected.

"Not in the daylight," she reminded him as she led the way. The blanket from home was lying in a heap. It smelled sour. Kicking it aside, Meg started to haul herself up the rope that was used to hoist hay off the wagon.

Paul shouted, "There's a car!"

Meg slid back and thumped onto the floor. Shoving past him, she barreled down the stairs and banged out the door. There was Dad's car, just pulling up toward the lodge.

"Dad!" she called as he emerged from the car.

He wheeled, looking thunderstruck, as both children rushed to him. "Meggie? Paul? What are you doing here?"

They hurled themselves at him, Paul wrapping his legs and arms around his father's leg, Meg jumping up and down and scrunching her father's sleeve in her hands.

"That was quick," Paul said. "Did you bring food? Where's Mom?"

"Your mother's in town." Dad spoke slowly, sounding puzzled. In the next moment it became clear that he and Orin had not crossed paths.

"Then what are you doing here?" Meg exclaimed.

"Checking on the lodge for Miss Trilling. Next I was going to pick up you two in Marks Mills. From where Mrs. Boudreau took you."

Paul frowned. "But we're here."

"I didn't know that. We'd better find Orin."

"Is everyone else all right?" asked Meg.

Dad nodded. "Even the cows. And we still have the barn. It's the only thing still standing on our road. The barn and ninety tons of hay."

"What about the house?" Meg asked.

Dad shook his head. "There's nothing but the chimney." He shook his head some more. "It's hard to take in. All our lumber's gone, too." He opened the back door of the car. "Lord!" he muttered as he ushered his children in.

"Are you mad?" Meg asked him. "Mad about everything burning?"

Sliding behind the wheel, he said, "Not mad. There's no point being mad."

Paul said, "I bet Uncle Frank is. He wants to get his hands on the guy that started the fire."

"Don't be silly," Dad replied as he backed the car and turned it up to the road. "Frank has other things on his mind."

But Paul didn't look convinced. Nor was Meg. She had no doubt that if ever Uncle Frank found out what Orin had done, he would kill him.

24 It didn't register about the house. It was unimaginable. Meg could tell that Paul didn't take it in either. Bit by bit, without sequence or order, their own story unfolded.

"We saw dead pigs," Paul informed his father. "June got burned, but she didn't die. We went swimming with our clothes on."

"We borrowed some of Miss Trilling's hay," Meg said.

"She has more than she needs for next summer. She'll probably want to share it with people that got burned out. I know we will."

"Is the fire over?" Paul asked.

"Hereabouts, yes. But it's still bad other places, like Mount Desert and Fryeburg. Real bad."

"Will you have to go away again?"

Dad shook his head. "I'm not sure. There's more firefighters now, experienced ones. It's equipment they're short of. That was the problem in Prescott Falls, but at least we kept the fire from jumping the river." He slowed. Up ahead a truck was turning in the road. As it came toward them, they saw Orin next to the driver.

Dad honked his horn. When the truck stopped, the driver and Dad spoke through open windows. The truck would take Orin back to the lodge so that he could ride June home.

"And my house flowers," Paul shouted across to Orin, who nodded without speaking because his mouth was full of sandwich.

"No," said Dad. "Leave the hens there."

"Orin's eating!" Paul exclaimed. "He's got food already. That's not fair."

The truck driver reached down on Orin's side and came up with three sandwiches wrapped in waxed paper. "Plenty more at the canteen," he said, handing them across to Dad.

The children gobbled, barely tasting the Spam and dry bread. They just chewed and chewed and swallowed.

When they reached the burn, familiar landmarks baffled them. Here was a roadside boulder Meg thought she knew, and yet there was nothing else around it to identify. So the boulder seemed out of place. As Dad slowed at the crossroad and Meg cast her eyes over smoldering foundations, she strained to recognize fields overspread with ash. Everything she saw on Meeting House Road tricked the eye. The backwoods stood broken and empty, so many charred bones splintering the smoky air.

It was eerie driving toward home. Even Paul was silenced. When Meg caught sight of Uncle Frank's truck off the road, it looked all wrong by itself. Ahead and to her left, nothing. No, there was the chimney, or part of it, amid the ruins of the house. Someone was poking around through the rubble. Aunt Helen? No, it was Gran, looking bulky in someone else's coat that was much too big for her.

As soon as Paul was out of the car, he started to run toward her. Then he stopped and retreated. "Where's Mom?" he asked in bewilderment.

"In town. Prescott Falls. I told you."

Paul backed away from Dad's outstretched hand. "Where's my swing?" he demanded.

Meg gazed at what was left of the great maple whose generous branches had shaded the dooryard every summer she could remember. She and Paul, Champ and Orin, and before them Mom and Uncle Frank, and even, Gran had claimed, Grampa—all had swung from its sturdiest bough. Not a trace of it remained but the trunk, split open and black.

Dad said, "The roots were still burning when we got here.

91

Joe Veazie knocked it down for us. He's here with his backhoe, helping."

"Where?" asked Paul.

"Behind the barn. You two stay here now. I'm going down to them." As he walked away, Aunt Helen climbed up from the hole around the chimney.

"What about my swing?" Paul called after his father.

"We'll make a new one," Dad answered, sounding drained.

Meg wondered what was the use of a swing without a tree to hang it from.

Aunt Helen and Gran seemed a long way off. Meg caught the surprise in their voices as Paul stumbled toward them over the ravaged ground. Maybe they weren't so far off after all. She heard Paul trying to explain what had happened, but they didn't understand, or else they didn't want to. Paul and Meg left behind? Impossible.

Meg didn't stir until Aunt Helen called to her. Then she started toward them without looking at where she was going. They shouted at her to watch out and then guided her around the treacherous cellar hole. Glancing down, she recognized nothing. A bitterness, not the earthy scent of carrots and potatoes, filled her nostrils.

They made her tell what had happened before the fire came. She spoke without feeling. She might have been describing a normal day in school. And she left out the part about Orin setting fire to the edge of the field. Instead she made sure that they understood that he had saved them.

"So where is he?" Aunt Helen demanded. When Meg said he was coming with June, Aunt Helen nodded. "He was supposed to go to the pond. That was the plan. He was supposed to go when we did, but he insisted on finishing the job he was at. He thought it could work, wetting along the field there." Aunt Helen rattled on, unable to stop reliving the decision to go on ahead of him to get to Charity Corners and pick up Meg and Paul. "I shouldn't've left him, but I had to get Sadie away from here. I didn't want her to see what was to come."

Gran snorted. "I knew what was coming, same as you. We had no business leaving that boy."

"He had the wagon, the team all hitched up," Aunt Helen retorted, defending her action as fervently as she had just blamed herself.

"He's Orin," Gran declared. "We should have seen to it that he left when we did."

"Even though he's all right? Even though he was here for Meg and Paul?"

"He's a boy," Gran said. "It was wrong."

The sparring wound down. Aunt Helen said to no one, to all of them, "Someone in a plane reported seeing a man and a horse. We figured he meant Orin, meant two horses. The report was called in from an airport phone. Lil got the word and sent someone to tell us that he was safe. There was no mention of any kids being with him. So when we found Toby here, we figured the report got most of it right."

"Toby's home?" Meg exclaimed.

Gran nodded. "He was at the barn. He's hurt bad. He'll have to be put down."

Aunt Helen, shaking her head, said, "Imagine you two being here yesterday. Imagine."

"What do you mean, put down?" Paul demanded.

Gran held him close and told him it would be cruel to keep Toby alive. "Some things have to be borne," she said, "like it or not." She gazed at the empty sky and said almost dreamily, "I will see our tree here, right here, till my last living day."

Paul pressed his face against her and covered his ears.

25 June announced her arrival while she was still on the road. From down by the barn Toby answered. Then June appeared with Orin, who slid from her back. Raising her head, she neighed again. Then she broke away from Orin and set off at a brisk trot.

"No, no," Aunt Helen called out, running toward Orin.

"It's all right," he told his mother. "She won't go anywhere. She just wants Toby."

Aunt Helen said, "Oh, Orin," but didn't go on.

Gran joined them, Meg and Paul in tow. "So you're all right," she declared. "Meg told us. We're proud of you, Orin."

Orin shook his head. "I lost the wagon, everything."

"You saved what matters most," Gran told him, "Meg and Paul and yourself."

He shook his head. "Didn't think Toby'd make it."

Aunt Helen drew a breath before telling him, "He didn't. He got himself home, that's all. He's bad off, Orin. Joe Veazie's here now digging a hole. He's going the rounds with his backhoe and shotgun. There's a lot of livestock beyond help, needing burying."

At first Orin didn't get it. "Didn't our cows make it out safe?"

Aunt Helen nodded. "Cows did." She placed a hand on his arm, and he sprang back as though burned.

Then it hit him. "Not Toby!" he yelled. "No, not Toby!" He lurched away down the hill.

"Don't," Aunt Helen shouted after him. "There's nothing you can do."

Meg started after him. She saw him stop once and cry out. She kept on, but he was way ahead of her. Now she could see Joe Veazie and Uncle Frank, but not her father, not June. Maybe Dad had taken June into the barn.

The next time Orin cried out, Uncle Frank turned for an instant. Then Meg saw Toby lying in the shadow of the barn. Uncle Frank stepped sideways and pointed the shotgun at Toby's upraised head. It seemed to Meg that Toby's legs thrashed before she actually heard the shot. He was on his side, galloping nowhere. There was another shot. After that Toby stopped moving. Uncle Frank handed the shotgun to Joe Veazie and turned abruptly from the horse. Meg thought he was coming to meet Orin, but then she realized that he was weaving from side to side as if he were blind and feeling his way, groping.

"You can't do that!" Orin shouted at him.

Tears streaming, Uncle Frank staggered right past him. Orin had to chase after his father, overtake him, and turn to confront him.

Uncle Frank slammed into Orin and then grabbed him, pinning Orin's arms, swaying with him. Orin, locked in his father's embrace, leaned back as far as he could.

Meg stood rooted, amazed at this slow-motion dance in the middle of the plowed field.

"He had no hoofs," Uncle Frank said.

"He came home, didn't he? Walked all the way home?"

Uncle Frank loosened his grip on Orin. "See for yourself then." He seemed to speak from the back of his throat. "See what Toby hobbled home on."

Aunt Helen reached them just as Orin took off. "Aren't you going after him?" she asked Uncle Frank.

He shook his head. "I have to get chains from the truck. We tried to get Toby to walk around below the barn to the hole, but he couldn't, so now we have to drag him. I can't do anything about Orin. Anyway, he won't let me. Never would." He wiped his hand across his face before going on.

Aunt Helen watched him trudge toward the truck. She met Gran halfway up the hill and said, "I guess Frank recollects how Orin never wanted to be held. Remember how he'd stiffen and pull away?"

Gran nodded. "I used to think we frightened him some way."

"And I guessed it was the colic. Champ was such an easy baby, I didn't know what colic was like. I kept waiting for Orin to grow out of it."

They stood together, looking down the hill at Orin, who knelt beside the lifeless horse. Meg's father came up behind him and bent down, his hand on Orin's shoulder. Meg wondered what Dad could say to comfort this unreachable boy. She had never heard Gran and Aunt Helen speak like this before. It wasn't that they didn't realize she was listening but that everything was altered now. For the first time some of the silence that had always surrounded Orin was broken.

A few minutes later Meg was surprised to see Orin help get the dead horse hitched for dragging below the barn. He seemed to go about the task as if it were all in a day's work.

When the job was done and after Joe had driven up the hill to knock down the chimney, the family gathered around the scattered bricks to consider what came next. By now everyone was hungry and thirsty. They decided that after they had unloaded a few things into the barn, Uncle Frank and Aunt Helen and Orin would go on over to Lerwick, where they would stay with Aunt Helen's brother. Gran would come with Dad and Meg and Paul to pick up Mom and get some food. Miss Trilling had sent word that the Yeadons could stay at the lodge if they needed a place, and Dad was anxious to settle in while there was still some daylight, since it was unlikely there would be any power this side of Charity Corners.

The last thing they did before leaving the farm was transfer a suitcase and a carton of clothes from the truck to the car. Then, when they were all ready, no one made the first move to go. Not that anything more could be done just then. Only it felt strange leaving like this.

"What about June?" Orin asked.

"I fed her," Meg's father told him. "She's best off inside with no one here and no fences left."

"She'll want Toby," Orin said.

"Toby," Gran repeated. "Named for October, the month he was born. And now the month he died in."

Uncle Frank opened the door of the cab. "Come on, old son," he said to Orin. "You'll have to squeeze in here between your mother and me."

The truck went first. Gran held back. Maybe there was something still needing to be tended to. But she was able to postpone going for only a minute or so. After all, there was nothing in all these bleak surroundings that she could fix or alter. For the first time in her life she was bereft of purpose.

26 As soon as they were on the road, Dad started telling the children what to expect. He explained that the tank truck and the pumper had come in time to save a good bit of Prescott Falls, even though they never made it this far west of town. But Meg and Paul had already seen Charity Corners, where there was no school, no houses, no barns. So Meg felt perfectly prepared already. By the time they reached the outskirts of town, she was thinking about seeing Mom and getting something to eat and drink.

Then she caught sight of the mill, and it took her breath

away. Its roof was gone, everything around it leveled and black. Yet buildings just beyond it appeared almost untouched.

When Dad drove by the town green, it looked to Meg as if some giant blade had sliced straight through it. At least the war memorial was still there. That must mean that Champ's name was there, too. Yet every house, every barn and garage on the north side of the green, the post office, Mr. Bowden's plumbing and heating business, and Bessie Barter's beauty parlor beside it were reduced to ashes and melted pipes.

Dad parked in front of the Grange. "I'll get Lil," he said

"I'm coming," Paul declared.

"No," Gran told him. "You two come inside with me for a meal."

"I want to see Mom," Paul pleaded.

But Gran was firm. She conducted the two children into the Grange Hall, which was crammed with people, some sitting at tables and eating, some pawing through donated clothes and blankets. Along the far wall a few men were stretched out on mattresses, some just sitting on the floor with their eyes closed.

Simon and Joyce pushed their way through to Meg. Everyone spoke at once, jabbering away about what they had seen and heard. Meg didn't tell them that her family's barn was undamaged. How could she speak of good fortune when their families had lost everything?

"You hear about Gus Browning?" Simon asked Meg.

She shook her head.

"They found him on Chimney Hill Road. Him and his old horse."

Meg could feel herself go hot and cold. Mr. Browning on the road with his horse just the way they had been with Toby and June?

Joyce said, "My father thinks he could've saved himself if

98

he hadn't tied the horse to the back of his old rattletrap truck. The horse couldn't keep up, or maybe it fell. Anyway, it got away, and he stopped to go after it. They think he had a heart attack. The horse probably died from the smoke."

Meg said, "Our horse Toby had to be shot."

Joyce said. "All our chickens burned. We don't know where the pigs are."

Meg did not reply.

Gran appeared, saying, "Food first. Talk after."

By then Paul was almost finished eating. So Meg sat at a table with neighbors and strangers all mixed up together. Someone handed her a plate of macaroni and cheese. It smelled better than Thanksgiving and Christmas combined. She shoveled it all in, washing it down with warm Coke that fizzed up her nose. She could have eaten a second plateful, but she didn't dare ask. When she carried her plate to the serving area, someone stuck a slice of apple pie on it. She ate it standing, wishing she could retrieve her paper cup for more Coke.

Gran reappeared and said she was going next door to Libby's Market. She would take Paul with her to keep him from going to look for his mother.

When Meg found Simon again, he asked about the lodge. He was astounded that she hadn't yet told her father that someone was inside. She said she hadn't had a chance to mention it yet. She couldn't inform Simon that she no longer believed in the spy or POW.

"Did you check the windows again?" he asked.

She shook her head. There hadn't been a sound from there last night or this morning, she told him.

"Still, he could be armed. You can't just let your family walk in there."

Speaking through an enormous yawn, Meg promised to warn them. She was full of macaroni and cheese and pie and

Coke. All she wanted now was for her mother to tuck her into bed somewhere safe.

Simon's escape had been too uneventful. No one had let him near the fire, and there hadn't been the slightest chance of facing danger heroically. He said, "Maybe I could go back with you. We're all so crowded at the Veazies'. I bet Miss Trilling has lots of rooms. Then I'd be on hand to help your dad."

Meg nodded. She figured that by tomorrow she'd be glad to have Simon there.

"What a break for all of you," Simon went on. "Miss Trilling couldn't get through on the telephone, so she called the state police to find your dad. Everyone's heard about it, how she made them do what she said. And now you have a fancy place to stay."

Meg said, "We'll ask if you can come."

They weaved their way to the door just as Meg's mother came through it. Meg flew to her. "You've been away forever," she shouted above the din. "Don't ever go again."

"I was here," Mom said to her. "You and Paul and Orin were the travelers. I can't get over what happened to you. And all the time we thought you were with the other kids from school. Where's Paul?"

"Gran took him with her to the store."

Mom said, "There's nothing left in there. Dad's bringing canned milk and peaches from the canteen. It's all they've got."

But even as she spoke, Gran and Paul came out of Libby's Market, Gran carrying a wooden box with some cartons and bags in it. Paul ran to his mother.

"Don't forget to ask," Simon reminded Meg.

But it was too confusing. Simon couldn't locate either of his parents, and when he suggested leaving a note for them on the Grange door the way Mrs. Boudreau had at school, that put an end to the whole idea. Meg's father, his arms full of cans, said, "No!" in a louder than usual voice, and Meg's mother declared, "Out of the question!"

"But—" Simon started to argue.

"No buts," Gran told him. "You won't find any of us paying heed to notes on doors, not ever again."

Simon cast a pleading glance Meg's way, but her head was buzzing. She could feel herself fading.

"Warn your father," Simon told her.

"What was that about?" Dad asked as he loaded the provisions into the car. Then he added, to no one in particular, "Never thought I'd be drinking canned milk."

"Or eating peaches from a factory," Gran retorted. "Not after all the jars of fruit I put up this year."

So Meg never got around to answering her father's question. She meant to, just to be on the safe side, although by now all notions of spies and POWs seemed to her like characters in a game of cops and robbers. Besides, if she mentioned Simon's suspicions in front of everyone, Gran would probably accuse Meg of stirring up trouble again, and then Dad would want to know why Meg had been at the lodge windows where she didn't belong.

27 It was nearly dark by the time Dad drove down Miss Trilling's driveway. Pulling up to the kitchen door, he left the headlights on.

Gran clutched herself as she stood waiting for Dad to unlock the door. "I'm glad we saved our winter coats," she remarked. "I wish I'd taken mine off the truck, though."

"The coats were on the wagon," Paul said to her.

"No, Paul. Helen and I packed the china in them. And a

good thing, too. See how nippy it gets when the sun goes down?"

"They were in front of the mattresses," Paul insisted. "Don't you remember?"

Mom put her arm around him and covered his mouth with her hand. "We'll unload the truck tomorrow, Ma," she said. "We'll sort everything out then."

Gran's muddle took Meg by surprise. She hung back, suddenly uneasy again. After all, she hadn't imagined the shadow moving behind the painted screen.

All of a sudden the lights came on. "Power!" Dad exclaimed.

The five of them crowded into the back entry. When he pushed open the door to the kitchen, they all just gaped, the grown-ups at the mess, the children at the gray, tiger-striped cat perched on the kitchen table. Stretching, she yowled as she rose to greet them. Two wild-eyed kittens, entwined in streamers of shredded toilet paper, struggled to free themselves.

"Miss Trilling's cat," Dad declared. "Now we know why she disappeared. It's lucky Miss Trilling had a hole cut beside the porch door in case the cat came back."

"Can we keep them?" Paul asked.

"I never did see any sign of her," Dad said.

"Can we, can we?" Paul begged.

No one answered him. Meg reached toward the kittens. One arched its back and hissed at her. The other scrambled away, dragging coils of toilet paper with it.

"This is my best place," Paul declared happily. "I never thought it was like this."

"Neither did I," Mom murmured as she began to gather up the toilet paper.

Dad walked through to the dining room, where more toilet paper was wound around the legs of the table and chairs. Bits of mouse feet and chipmunk tails, feathers, and bird legs littered the floor. Right behind her father, Meg gazed with wonder at the array of animal heads mounted high on the wall. Buffalo and elk and other imposing beasts seemed unwilling to look down upon such tawdry leavings. What a stir one cat and her kittens could make. Meg wasn't the least sorry to have found them behind the mystery of the moving shadow instead of a spy or POW. But Simon was bound to feel let down.

"Don't try cleaning up tonight," Dad advised. "We're all worn out." He led the way up the back stairs to two small rooms and a bathroom. Everyone followed in hushed amazement, feeling the scrolls carved on the stair rail, and gazing at the glass shades covering the wall lights.

The stairs turned and rose again to the attic, which was vast, even though a kind of room without a door jutted out into the middle of the space. Meg guessed it boxed in a secret closet, but Dad said that it surrounded the entrance hall and main stairway, which were open from the ground floor all the way to the roof. This side of the attic, he told her, used to be the bedroom for the maids. Huge domed trunks lined one wall. Closet doors opened to reveal shelves of wrapped bedding and clothes bags hanging in neat rows. They smelled of cedar.

The grown-ups decided to let the children sleep here if they promised not to touch anything in the closets.

"It's too dark," Paul protested.

"But wait till morning," Mom said. "I bet it will be all rosy when the light comes through the colored glass." She showed him the small, ornate dormer windows. "We'll make your bed on the floor right here, so you'll see it first thing."

"Like camping out," Meg told him, warming to the idea of this strange place.

"I just did camp out. Last night. I was cold."

Gran nodded. "Paul's right," she declared. "There must be many more beds in this house. What's wrong with putting them to use?"

But Mom and Dad were already unrolling some of the old carpets they found stored under the eaves. "There's all kinds of precious things in every room," Dad explained. "Everything's breakable." He went downstairs to get a lightbulb. When it was screwed into a socket on one of the crossbeams, the attic took on a friendlier look. Dad attached a string to the short chain and ran it down to the makeshift carpet beds. Now Meg and Paul had their own light. Mom said they could keep it on, just tonight. By the time Dad had turned on the water and the children had used the bathroom and climbed back up to the attic, the beds were all made with pillows and blankets.

Mom stayed with them for a few minutes. She wanted to hear their own accounts of their escape from the fire. But Paul fell asleep almost at once.

Meg treasured this time alone with her mother. "If Orin did something bad," she finally asked, "and after that was really good, would that undo the bad thing?"

Mom couldn't tell without knowing more. She said she supposed by now she had heard all about the good. She would have to consider the bad as well.

Meg didn't know how to go on. She longed to tell Mom about Orin setting the fire. But all of Champ's vague warnings weighed on her: how most people tended to blame Orin when something went wrong, even if he wasn't guilty. This time he was; he had started the fire at the farm. How could she protect him now that the deed was done? Could she risk exposing him even to Mom? Uncle Frank was Mom's older brother. If Meg told her everything, Mom might feel she had to inform him.

"Uncle Frank shot Toby," Meg said.

"I know," Mom replied. "He had no choice."

"He cried. Uncle Frank cried."

"Yes."

Meg sat up. "Did you know that?"

Mom shook her head. "But it doesn't surprise me."

"Did you know that he called Orin old son?"

Mom drew Meg into her arms and rocked her. "You're afraid that he'll change about Orin just when he's beginning to find him? Because of the bad thing?"

Meg nodded. "If he finds out."

Mom didn't speak right away. Finally she said, "Then let it go." She pulled away from Meg. "There's tough times ahead. We don't need to borrow trouble where Orin's concerned."

Meg shivered. Mom pushed her down and pulled the blanket over her.

"Champ made me promise to look after Orin," Meg murmured.

"You've done that. Too much. Orin has to get along the best he can."

"He took care of us yesterday," Meg said. "He really saved us."

"Let him be a hero then," Mom said to her. "Orin needs that more than anything. So do Frank and Helen."

Meg sighed. "Don't go," she whispered. But it was she who slipped away from her mother now, drifting into sleep.

28 In the morning the attic looked different and wonderful. There were a couple of old chairs and a cradle Meg hadn't noticed the night before. There were nooks and corners like secret hideaways. And there were blue and red and yellow streams of sunshine that shimmered on the floor beneath the colored windows.

Downstairs all the unrolled toilet paper and remnants of birds and mice had been cleaned up. Mom had even let the hens out of the stable, and Dad had already left for his mail delivery.

"I thought the post office burned up," Meg said.

"It did," Mom told her. "But the train will still bring mail."

Meg wondered how Dad would find people who had no homes anymore. He couldn't just leave the letters under a brick next to a cellar hole.

Gran switched on the radio. She hushed the children, saying they should all listen to the news and count their blessings. So they heard how Mount Desert had lost power after the fire reached the hydroelectric transformer and how the Fryeburg fire had sprung to life yet again and now threatened the neighboring town of Brownfield. Fifty fires still burned in Maine. Gran turned off the news before it was finished.

They ate cornflakes with canned peaches and evaporated milk. When Paul poured some milk into his empty dish and set it down on the floor for the cat and kittens, Mom told him they couldn't spare people food for animals until the crisis was over.

"Crisis?" said Paul. "Is that a swearword?"

"Emergency," Mom told him. "Shortage."

Paul mulled that for a moment and then asked, "Will we ever go to school again?"

"Of course," said Mom and Gran together. But neither of them could tell him anything more than that.

The mother cat led her kittens to the dish on the floor. They followed her example, dipping mouths to milk. One sputtered, spraying milk, and the other sneezed and then leaped sideways, twisting in midair and landing its hind end in the milk. The cat tongued its dripping hindquarters and then went back to lapping from the dish.

The kittens gave up trying to drink and went sliding about on the milky linoleum. Gran scowled and then, in spite of herself, couldn't keep from laughing at their antics. Paul laughed, too, but when he dropped to the floor to join in their game, they hissed and retreated, leaving a trail of tiny white paw prints in their wake.

"Give them time," Mom told him. "We must be the first people they've ever seen."

"Grace and Disgrace will help," Paul responded. "They'll teach them how to get along with people."

"But no hens in this house," Mom told him. "Remember, we're visitors here."

Dad showed up before noon with more supplies and news. The Red Cross was setting up a real relief center in town. The Coventry dump had caught fire during the night, but it was under control now.

Dad was going back to see if more volunteers were needed there. Mom decided to go with him. She could help out at the canteen until the telephone crews repaired enough lines to put the exchange back in business. On the way Gran and the children could be dropped off at the farm.

"Who'll take care of me?" Paul asked.

"Gran," said his mother. "And you'd better mind her."

107

"Why can't you—" He broke off under her glowering look.

"What will we do at the farm all day?" Meg asked.

"Make yourself useful," said her mother.

"Stay out of the way," said her father.

"Why don't we just stay here?" Meg demanded. She longed to explore the attic.

But there were more reasons than her parents wanted to recite, although Dad did point out that since most of the lodge was off limits to the Yeadon family, there would be even less to do around here than at the farm.

Meg didn't believe this for a second, but she managed to choke back a retort about his strict house rules that Gran had already challenged. Meg figured that maybe if she behaved, they would let Simon come to stay for a while.

Silently Meg began to muster her arguments.

29 Uncle Frank and Aunt Helen and Orin were down at the springhouse. Pete Kresky had come over to help repair the roof and frame, which must have been hit by a flying ember. They kept traipsing up to the barn in search of spare lumber and then ended up dismantling Toby's stall for its heavy planks.

When the tractor broke down, Orin harnessed June to the stoneboat to haul the wood. As soon as she was backed between the shafts and hooked to the singletree, she started to toss her head and neigh. Meg, who stood at her head, stroking her blistered nose, asked Orin if she was fussing because it hurt her to wear the harness over her burns.

"How should I know?" he snapped. Meg winced. Pushing her aside, he snatched the reins from her. Then he said, "She's calling Toby."

"It's not my fault," she blurted.

"What isn't?"

"Whatever you're mad at," she told him.

June, quiet now, rubbed her chin on his shoulder.

"It's me I'm mad at," he said. He stared down at the ground.

Hoping he would finally mention starting the fire, she pressed him to explain.

But he only said, "Toby. My fault."

That made no sense to her. "You did the best you could," she insisted. "There wasn't time for both horses."

"I took too long here. Made us late."

"Why, Orin? Why did you do it?"

He spread his arms, describing the extent of the plowed field. "You saw" was all he answered. "I had to. Had to try. That's what Champ always says. Try."

She couldn't figure out how he could blame himself for losing Toby and not blame himself for the fire. "Who else knows?" she asked warily.

"Huh?" Then he added, "What difference does it make?"

She didn't answer. How could she hope to unload the secret they shared, when he was so unaware of what could happen to him if the truth about the fire came out? Finally she said, "I guess you feel bad because you did a bad thing."

He nodded. "Guess so."

"Orin!" shouted his father. "You coming?"

"Yup," he called back. He spoke to Meg. "See, the field was plowed. So I had a chance. I tried like Champ says to. I didn't think. Only about the barn." He clucked to June, and she leaned into her collar.

Meg stumbled through the rough, dry earth to keep up with them. "What about the barn?" she asked Orin.

He stopped so short that she bumped into him. June lifted her muzzle and neighed again. "See for yourself," he told her almost angrily. "It's here. Toby isn't."

In one more attempt to get him to explain about the fire, Meg said, "Aunt Helen and Gran thought you were watering the edge of the field."

Orin shrugged. "They'd never've let me start any fire. Gran, she does sometimes think I can do things. But she worries what'll happen. Champ never worries. He says it can't hurt to try." Orin shook his head. "So I did. No harm trying. The big fire was almost here." His voice dropped. "Only there was harm. I took too long." He kept shaking his head. "Champ says . . . Where is he? I want Champ."

Meg was more baffled than ever. "Champ's dead," she told him. "Orin, you know that."

He shook his head. "Toby's dead. He's in the ground, down behind the barn. Grampa's dead. Buried. There's a stone over him."

Meg lowered her voice to match his. "Champ's dead, too. It happened far away. They couldn't send him home."

"Why not?"

The answer arranged itself in words Meg couldn't utter: *Blown to bits*. Her mind went blank. She didn't want to be the oldest one, didn't want to keep Orin's secret. She didn't want to know more than Orin or more about him than anyone else.

"Where is he then?" Orin pleaded, fixing her for once with a direct look.

Seeing the confusion and pain in his eyes, Meg could almost hear the kids at school who used to taunt him, naming him the Great Stone Face. And she knew that she was stuck with him, not just because she had promised Champ but because Orin had let her see where he was hurt.

"Champ's on the town green," she said. "He's not buried there, like Grampa in the graveyard, but his name is carved in the stone. You've seen it. You know which one it is. It's there because Champ was killed."

"Orin!" Uncle Frank shouted. "Get a move on."

As June lurched forward, Meg fell behind. Probably she would never know much more than she had learned just now. Orin had shown her that he did blame himself for the fire. In a way. But would he even have thought about it afterward if he hadn't seen Toby with his hoofs burned off?

She stood midway between the barn and the springhouse and watched Uncle Frank and Pete Kresky stoop to help Orin unload the stoneboat. He was as big as the grown-ups. They looked like three men working together.

She wondered whether Orin would ever feel one with them. Or was he bound to be different for the rest of his life?

30 Within the next few days burned-out families moved into cabins made available by summer residents. Meg kept hoping that the Leblancs and Farrises would come, but they made other temporary arrangements, and Simon didn't even get to visit. At least Paul had some kids to play with, and Meg earned a little money keeping an eye on them.

That left Gran alone for long stretches of time. She took to muttering or just moving her lips as if conversing silently with herself. When Meg came running in one afternoon to tell her it had begun to rain, Gran merely nodded. In her excitement Meg raced out to feel this first rain wash over her, but it just dribbled down as if wrung from the dingy sky. Coming back inside, she had nothing to show for the shower but wet clothes. Gran didn't even bother to make her change.

When telephone service was restored, Mom made a point of calling to check in, but after a while Gran stopped hearing the phone ring. Usually Meg answered it for her, but once she was in the bathroom when it rang and Paul ran to pick it up. She assumed he was speaking to Mom until she heard him ask if he could keep the house flowers in the lodge. By the time Meg got to the phone, Paul was hanging up.

He gave her his sunniest smile and said, "Miss Trilling says she likes house flowers."

"You can't," Meg scolded. "She didn't understand."

"She does, too. She says we can keep one kitten. She's going to help everyone in Charity Corners. It's a surprise, so don't tell."

But Paul told everyone about Miss Trilling letting Grace and Disgrace into the house. When Mom shook her head, Paul insisted. "She said if they lived through the fire, they deserved a home."

"Sure," muttered Dad, "maybe stuffed and mounted on the wall."

"They have a home in the stable," Mom pointed out. "Besides, I doubt that Miss Trilling realizes we're not using the whole house. The kitchen is also our parlor."

But later, after Miss Trilling had called again and spoken with Dad, the hens moved into the back entry. Mostly when they were indoors, they were caged. Whenever they did get out, they terrorized the kittens, who in turn bedeviled the two small hens.

Gran took little notice of these skirmishes. Even when Grace and Disgrace peeped imploringly for tidbits, her hands remained in her lap, and no crumbs were brushed to the floor.

Everyone tried to interest her in doings at the farm, but nothing seemed to matter to her, not even the cows coming home or the arrival of one of the prefab houses made available to fire victims. Uncle Frank thought that she would get back to normal once she was living at home again. But she refused to set foot inside the "tin house," rejecting the very idea that such a temporary building could be home.

When Meg was with Gran, she felt sad for her, but when she was off in the woods or alone in the attic, she felt free from worry about anything or anyone.

Then one day she came home to find the kitchen empty. Her first thought was that Gran was better and was outside doing something useful like taking in the clothes. Meg went to check. The wash was still on the clothesline, even though a sharp wind was blowing icy mist in from the pond. She knew that it was up to her to rescue the laundry before it got wet, but she ran back inside instead and up the stairs. Gran wasn't in either room or in the bathroom.

Meg was on the back stairs when she heard a kind of humming through the wall. Humming or moaning? She tore down to the kitchen, through the dining room, and across the front hall. Gran was in the parlor, its heavy curtains drawn and no lights on.

"I didn't know where you were," Meg told her, groping for a light switch.

Gran slowly turned. She clutched herself as if in pain.

"Are you all right?" Meg asked her.

"I can't find Orin," Gran said. "I'm so worried for him. I can tell something's wrong. I came all this way, and now I can't get back. Do you think he's lost, too?"

Meg found the light and turned it on. Gran blinked and looked all about her in surprise. There were paintings in golden frames. There were bronze figures and a marble statue and a silvery gazing ball that reflected Gran's face swollen out of shape.

Meg took Gran's hands, which were freezing. "Orin's with Eddie," Meg said, "working in the woods. He'll be here Sunday." She started to lead Gran back to the kitchen. At least Gran was talking, even if she didn't make much sense.

"I worry about Orin when I can't see him," Gran explained. "You never know," she added as she sat down in the kitchen

113

chair Meg pulled out for her. "You wonder what will become of him. Did you say he's here?"

"He will be," Meg told her. "Sunday."

"He gets frostbite, you know. He doesn't notice in time. I like to make sure that he's dressed for the cold."

Meg put on the kettle and made them cups of tea. Gran talked on for a while, her conversation wandering. At least she was calmer now. What bothered Meg was that there was nothing in Gran's manner that recognized Meg as her granddaughter. She might have been any neighbor who had casually dropped in for a chat.

It was strange to be cut off this way, especially when Meg was already so alone out here. There was no one her age around, and Paul was usually with the younger kids. She had spoken with Joyce a couple of times and had met Simon once in front of Libby's Market. Not for a minute did he believe that a cat and two kittens could have made the shadow they had seen. He wasn't just disappointed; he was disgusted because Meg had let the real intruder slip away.

She guessed that Simon was still annoyed at having missed out on the fire, but she expected everything would get back to normal as soon as they were together at school again. Then when word came that the older kids from Charity Corners would be bused to the Prescott Falls junior high school, where room was being made for them, she was too anxious about the move to look forward to being with her friends.

"I'm not old enough for junior high," Meg told her mother. "They wear different clothes in junior high." She envied Paul, who would be going to school in the Grange with just the kids he already knew and Miss Wylie.

Mom reminded her that next year, when the addition was completed, Meg and her classmates were due to shift over to that school anyway.

So a new routine was established during the week, while

114

every Sunday the whole family gathered in the lodge kitchen for midday dinner. This was supposed to give Gran something to do and look forward to, but usually Meg's mother ended up doing the cooking. Gran would start something and then wander off, picking at a thread or a spot on her apron that no one else could see.

Orin, who worked in the woods cutting and stacking salvage timber from trees that couldn't survive the underground root damage, was always hungry and almost always as silent as Gran. But Meg noticed him watching Gran. He looked as if he were waiting, as if he expected her to speak up in her old, forthright way. But while Gran glanced his way from time to time, she seemed at a loss to understand what he was doing in this strange kitchen, so far from where they both belonged.

Uncle Frank felt sure that Gran would want to make butter again. "I've requested a new churn," he informed her one Sunday. "The Red Cross said they'd try to get one."

Gran turned up her hands, empty.

In her mind's eye, Meg saw the remains of the glass churn after the fire, the twisted handle, everything melted.

"Well, anyhow, Ma," Frank went on, "you'll want to be home next weekend when we stake out the new foundation. We may get it poured before hard frost."

Gran turned her hand down and then up again.

"So will you come?" he asked.

She gave a slight nod and sucked in her breath. "I imagine," she answered.

Uncle Frank dug into his mashed potatoes, and the talk turned to the donated furniture he had picked up in Coventry, some for the Kreskys and some for the Grays and Yeadons. The Kreskys were the first people on the road to receive a delivery of army surplus building materials, and most of the neighbors were working to get their new little house framed and roofed before the first serious snowfall.

"How about it?" Uncle Frank asked, turning to Orin. "You going to help us put the house up?"

"Dunno," Orin replied through a mouthful of mashed potato.

"At least he and Eddie are getting paid for their work in the woods," Mom said.

"Is that it?" Uncle Frank asked. "You like the money?"

Orin shrugged. "Lots of work out there."

"Still, think about it. It's not often you get to learn a trade like that right at home."

"Home," echoed Gran, then said no more.

Meg stole a glance at Orin. Was he glad his father wanted him or afraid he couldn't measure up? Did he think about the fire anymore? Maybe he had nightmares. About kerosene and its dancing flames? About Toby's burned feet? She couldn't begin to guess. No more could she imagine how this fractured family would shatter if Orin's secret were revealed.

31 That night, after wondering whether Orin ever had nightmares, Meg had one herself. It began in the central hall of the lodge, which was supposed to be off limits. But sometimes Meg went there anyway just to wade through the colors that spilled down from the tinted panes of the star-shaped skylight.

That was how her dream began. She was trying to catch the reds and blues and yellows as they slipped through her fingers like water. A distant voice came to her, calling her from danger. But she stayed. She wasn't doing any harm, was she? "Come," called the voice while she spread her hands and then cupped them to hold those amazing colors. "Hurry," urged the voice, closer now and familiar. All at once she recognized the voice. It was her own, and it called her away from flames that blazed up from the blues and reds and yellows. They surrounded her, snapping sparks and darting every which way like frenzied demons.

She woke up in a sweat, her body clenched and aching. She had to sit in the darkness awhile to sort out what was dream from what was real.

Suddenly Paul spoke up. She hadn't even realized he was awake. "Everyone talks about the fire," he said. "Why don't you?"

"Because I'm sick of it," she told him. "It's over."

"Do you think it's fair?" he asked.

"Think what's fair?" It was comforting to be talking like this. It felt normal. She lay back down and pulled up the covers.

"Fair that this house that nobody lives in didn't burn and ours did."

"Miss Trilling lives here in the summer," Meg reminded him.

Paul was silent a moment. Then he said, "Two families lived in our house. Lots of people."

"Well," Meg answered through an enormous yawn, "that's just the way it is." She was ready to go to sleep now. The nightmare had receded.

"What will Uncle Frank do if he finds out that Orin started the fire?"

Meg's breath caught in her throat. Paul knew! And all this time he had never said a word about it. Rolling onto her stomach, she raised herself up on her elbows. "Don't you ever mention that," she whispered fiercely.

"Why? Would Uncle Frank kill him?"

"Of course not," Meg retorted.

"He said he would," Paul shot back. "He said if he ever caught the guy that started the fire, he'd wring his neck."

"There were lots of fires," Meg responded lamely. "Some just happened. Anyway, it's not all Orin's fault."

"How come?"

"The big fire was already practically there. That's why everyone left."

"Oh," said Paul, sounding unconvinced. But he had run out of questions. In a few minutes he was sound asleep.

Meg was wide-awake now. She found herself trying to recall everything about the fire and all that led up to it. She kept backing up and backing up until she was here at Charity Pond that Sunday before. The shadows moving behind the painted screens could have been made by someone who lit fires just for the thrill of it and didn't care what damage they did. What if that dangerous person was caught and punished? Then it wouldn't matter so much what Orin had done.

Or would it?

She backed up again. Suppose there hadn't been a cat and kittens making the shadows, but a person. Who would hide here? Sleepily her mind played with a new possibility. What if the person hiding had been Champ? Maybe the army just thought he was killed but he had gone AWOL instead. Maybe he was here in the lodge, waiting for the right time to show up.

But would Champ desert? Meg shook her head. He might plan to escape from the farm, he might decide to head for Portland or even Boston, but that was different. Running out on his family was not the same as running away from the army.

Meg shuddered, hugged herself, and wished she could unthink such a horrible thought about her dead cousin.

If only he hadn't planned to abandon Orin. Hadn't he realized that Orin would always rely on him to push back the invisible walls that hemmed him in? If Meg could see this now, why hadn't Champ? Orin needed so much more than

118

someone to fight his tormentors. Yet Champ had exacted a promise from Meg long before she could have understood that it wasn't enough. It had never been enough.

Thinking back to Champ's last day at home, when he had caught her on the swing in midflight, she wondered whether she would have had the strength to set him straight if she had known then what she now understood. Would it have made any difference? Or would Champ even have bothered to hang around long enough to hear her out?

Probably not. He had just set himself free. He had squared things away the best he could. And now he could never release Meg from that promise.

Talk about fair and unfair. All you had to do to be a hero was to get yourself killed. Run off and leave your brother and your cousin and never come back.

If only she could confide in one person. Before the fire that would have been Simon, who was as good at keeping secrets as she was. But they never had a chance to talk anymore.

Just being in school with older kids changed everything. The boys didn't mix with the girls now. All you had to do was be seen talking to a boy and everyone would assume you were chasing after him. If there had been any way to get together on weekends, the old friendships might have revived. But not one of Meg's friends had a bike anymore. Besides, few of them were living where they used to. And across the river in Prescott Falls everything in junior high was as rigid and pre-cast as the concrete blocks that made its walls.

Meg sighed. She had lost track of her recollections, had muddied them with her fantasy about Champ hiding out in the lodge. At least she had rejected that crazy notion almost as quickly as she had concocted it.

Now, at last, she allowed herself to think about her dream. How she had longed to catch those colors. Was that before they turned into flames? It was weird the way something so beautiful could in an instant be changed. Maybe that was how Orin saw fire. Maybe it had nothing to do with his craving danger.

She supposed she would never really know what had made him set that fire. It was hard enough trying to figure out her own feelings, especially when those fluid dream colors turned to flames.

But it was a dream, she had to remind herself. And it was common knowledge that dreams turned things inside out.

32 Just before Thanksgiving Orin came to terms with the fact that June couldn't work anymore. Her lungs seemed to have given out. Orin maintained that when she was teamed up with another horse, she worked herself into such a lather that she fell into a coughing fit. But everyone else except Meg figured that June had never recovered from all the smoke she inhaled during the fire.

Meg guessed that the trouble was at least as much Orin's, that he couldn't bear June's constant grieving for Toby. He still went on timbering, though. He also helped out from time to time on the Kreskys' house, but it was never easy for him and his father to work together for long. Orin's botched measurements usually showed up in uneven lengths and misfitting joints.

Every weekend the Yeadons took Gran to the farm to see the progress on the foundation for the small house that was to replace the big one that was gone. While she never failed to greet Zac like an old friend, she showed little interest in anything else. Most of the time she just gazed past the foundation to the scorched and naked land beyond.

Meg kept hoping that Orin would be around. But even when he turned up, they were never really together so that Gran could keep track of him the way she used to in the farmhouse kitchen.

So what else was Gran attached to? Meg searched her memory for anything that might draw Gran out of her deep silence. Recalling what Gran had said about her own mother never entirely settling in after she had left the house with the apple trees to move into the farm, Meg thought of Gran's sampler. If Meg could find it, maybe Gran would start talking again about when she was a girl, like when her mother made her pull out all the red apples and make the maple tree in the sampler true. But Mom had no idea what had become of that scrap of cloth with its faded cross-stitching. It could be anywhere. Or nowhere.

Eventually Meg nagged Aunt Helen into remembering that Gran had slipped a few folded mementos into her coat pockets before the coats were packed on the wagon. "Don't mention things that got burned," Aunt Helen told Meg. "You'll only make matters worse. Haven't you anything to do besides minding other people's business?"

So Meg had to think of something away from Aunt Helen, like bringing Zac to the lodge to keep Gran company. Her parents didn't tell her to tend to her own business, but they said it was out of the question. Uncle Frank needed Zac for the cows, and besides, Miss Trilling wouldn't want another animal in her already crowded kitchen.

Although Meg could see that Zac's company wasn't really what was needed, she started to argue. Miss Trilling was far away in Florida, so why should she care if her kitchen was crowded? Anyway, she had made it clear that she approved of pets. That was why she had come up with the idea of a show of pet survivors to give the local children a part in the fund-raiser that was supposed to boost everyone's spirits, bring the community together, and help restore some of the town's failed services.

Since Mom and Dad couldn't dispute Miss Trilling's thoughtfulness and generosity, they just shook their heads and said no.

Even though Miss Trilling couldn't come north for the big event, she was organizing out-of-state contributors, and she had expressed a keen interest in the newspaper's sponsorship of an award for a young hero of the fire.

A reporter had already come nosing around, interviewing people about what he called the inferno. Pretty soon everyone knew that he was scouting out candidates for the award. Several of the high school boys who had joined the firelines were being considered. He said their stories would appear later in the paper.

The reporter even came to the junior high school to ask kids about their fire experiences. Nathan Mills's sister, Marilyn, was a contender for the young hero award because she had stopped to rescue old Mrs. Spofford's three-legged dog. The newspaper carried a picture of her. People wrote in urging that she win since she couldn't compete in the pet show because the dog wasn't hers. Besides, what kinds of tricks could you teach a three-legged dog?

"Grace and Disgrace don't know any tricks either," Paul said to Meg. "Joan Barter says I can't take them in the pet show because chickens are dumb clucks."

"Joan's just trying to spoil the show for you. She's probably jealous because she doesn't have a pet."

"Still," Paul insisted, "there's supposed to be tricks, and we don't have any."

"The kittens are tame enough to train now," Meg said. "Maybe you could take the smartest one."

Paul shook his head. "It has to be pets that were almost in the fire."

"Zac then."

Paul brightened. "Zac lies down when I tell him. Is that a good trick?"

Meg nodded, thinking Joan must figure she could get away with just about anything now that Paul's older sister was in a different school.

Paul continued to worry. When the reporter came to the lodge to talk to the Yeadons and Gran, Paul even asked him how important tricks were for the pet show. The reporter said that he would try to find out but that right now he was working on something else.

As soon as he made it clear that Orin was the focus of his attention, Meg's heart sank. So she was relieved that Paul was distracted.

When it was her turn to be questioned, she told the reporter how Orin had taken her and Paul into the culvert under the bridge. The reporter said the judges, who were the newspaper editor and important people in town that he called the town fathers, had gotten wind of this already. He had been sent to gather more details.

Meg talked and talked so that Paul wouldn't get a word in edgewise. Not that it was necessary. Paul was utterly absorbed in the house flowers and whether he would be able to show them. Just now he had thoughts for little else.

33 A few days later the reporter showed up again, this time when the family was at supper. Invited to join the Yeadons and Gran, he joked that the local folks ought to put out a macaroni cookbook with all the different ways it could be prepared. Since cases of it had been distributed by the Red Cross to area fire victims, it was dished up at almost every meal. Probably he was offered macaroni everywhere he went. Meg's mother replied that she doubted that any of them would want to think about macaroni, let alone eat it, ever again. Or Spam. And Paul said, "Do you remember corn on the cob?" Everyone laughed.

"Is that your favorite?" the reporter asked him.

Paul nodded. "And turkey. And blueberry pie."

Even Gran was roused into nodding approval.

Then the reporter turned to Meg and said, "Tell me about the backfire out at the farm."

Meg blinked.

Her father said, "Backfire?"

The reporter spread out a map of the area and jabbed at a spot with the tip of his pencil. "That your barn?"

Dad nodded.

"Someone started a backfire. The pilot who told me said there was just one man. I know you weren't there. Frank Gray wasn't either. He was on the road to Lerwick with his cows. The women took off in the truck. That would be you, Mrs. Gray, and your daughter-in-law. Right?" He was looking at Gran.

She looked back. "I imagine," she answered after a quick intake of breath.

Meg held herself as still as she could. Maybe the reporter

would drop the question. She began to think about how to change the subject.

But her parents were fixing her with looks, too. There was no way to dodge their intense interest.

"Who was the man?" the reporter asked.

Meg shook her head. "I . . . We were in the house. Looking for the hens."

"What's going on?" her father demanded. "You're hiding something."

She stared at her plate of macaroni. White worms, she thought. Fat white worms. She was afraid she was going to throw up.

The reporter swung around to Paul, but Dad beat him to the next question. "Was anyone else at the farm besides you and Meg and Orin?"

Paul said, "No." Then he added, "Except Grace and Disgrace and Toby and June. They were all there, too."

Meg couldn't bring herself to look at Paul. He had no idea that he had just condemned his cousin.

Dad pressed on. "Orin started a fire?"

Paul glanced at Meg. Then he pushed away from the table and ran to the back stairs. They heard him pounding up to the attic.

Meg's mother stood. Then she hesitated.

"Sorry," said the reporter. "I didn't mean to cause a ruckus. I tried to speak to Orin Gray about this, but he wouldn't talk about the fire at all." When no one replied, he added lamely, "It's an unusual situation."

Ignoring him, Meg's father said, "Meg, you'd better speak up."

"I can't," Meg said between clenched teeth. "I promised Champ."

"What's it got to do with Champ?" Dad demanded.

"I promised," Meg whispered.

"You're not making sense," he snapped.

"Mike, don't," Meg's mother told him. "I think I know what this is about." She leaned toward Meg. "This was the bad thing you wanted to talk about. Right?"

Meg sucked in a breath, trying not to cry. She nodded.

"Oh, Meggie, I'm so sorry."

Meg turned to the reporter. "Will Orin go to prison?"

"Prison!" Gran exclaimed, drawing herself up. "Is that what Orin thinks? Who put that idea in his head? This is more of your fire in the wind, isn't it? Don't you know better than to meddle with that boy?"

Meg wanted to protest that she wasn't the one who was stirring up trouble; it was the reporter. But she didn't dare open her mouth. She was afraid of what else might come out, afraid of what already had. She no longer saw white worms on her plate, only Orin spilling a trail of kerosene along the edge of the plowed field. She saw the woods smoking and the sky like night. She saw Orin retracing his steps, stooping once and then again and once more after that. She couldn't save him from what he had done. She could almost hear that fire train bearing down on him. Nothing would stop it now. It would roar right over him.

"He's sorry," Meg tried to tell them. "He feels awful, because of Toby. Because it took so much time."

"No, Meg, no," Mom said. She reached across the table for Meg's hand. But it was clenched in a fist, and Meg couldn't open it, couldn't move.

Dad said, "Orin lit a backfire? How could he do that all by himself?" Dad sounded stunned. "A backfire's desperate hard to control. How could one boy, especially Orin, do such a thing?"

The reporter was writing on his spiral pad.

Gran spoke in a small, withered voice. "He was down there

with the milk can. We told him he couldn't possibly carry enough water in it to stop a fire. That's what we thought he was pouring out. Water."

"He was doing that when you left?" the reporter asked.

Gran nodded. "We said to come. He said he'd be right along. We had less time because we were heading for Charity Corners. So was the fire. So we left him." Her words were like dried-out husks. She dropped her head in her hands and sat for a moment, bent over, silent. Then she straightened. When she spoke again, she sounded almost angry. "We were stopping for the children at school. That's where we thought they were. But I knew we shouldn't leave him alone, even though we didn't have an inkling of what he was really up to."

The reporter asked Gran what had come into her mind when she found the school empty. Relief, she told him, since that meant Paul and Meg were already away and safe. In spite of her misgivings, she had supposed Orin was safe, too. The wind was still out of the northwest, and Orin was to drive the team west and then south and east to the pond. That was the long way around, but it was supposed to be open.

Meg recalled something she had forgotten until now: how the wind had suddenly stopped blowing. It had been in that instant of stillness that she had hollered at Orin to hurry and he had waved her silent. It had been only a matter of seconds before the air was aswirl with leaves and bits of hay and grass. She hadn't seen Orin strike the first match. She hadn't even realized he was lighting the fire until it was well along the border of the plowed field. The wind had sprung up at the same moment the flames had leaped into life. It had seemed as if each fed the other.

"The wind changed," she said.

The reporter nodded. "The pilot saw it veer around. It didn't last. He saw the new fire start to race toward the woods. He couldn't stay to watch it meet up with the main fire. The visibility was lousy and getting worse. So he yelled at the guy to get out of there. Then he took off."

Gran moaned. It was like the sound she had made when Meg had found her lost in Miss Trilling's parlor.

"It's all right, Ma," Meg's mother said. "Orin's all right."

Gran's breath caught. "Oh, Lil, I felt all along that something had him all churned up. Yes, and more than somewhat. But I couldn't tell what."

"You're not to blame," Meg's mother said. "I'd told Meg about Orin. Then I stopped her telling about . . . this."

But Gran shook her head. "I gave up on the boy. Because there was no place to be like always. We needed somewhere to sit awhile and talk. I gave up on him."

"I'm sure you did everything you could," the reporter said to her.

Gran responded to his attempt to comfort her with a slight nod that was just short of rude.

Meg's mother came around to Meg. "I can see why you thought what Orin did was bad." She glanced at the reporter. "Because of what I'd told you about him," she added warily. "But why was Paul scared to tell us?"

Meg felt bound to her chair. It didn't seem to matter what she said now that the worst was out. "Paul's afraid because of what Uncle Frank said he'd do to anyone that started a fire."

"But this was different," the reporter tried to explain. "Don't you understand?"

"No," Meg answered, tears streaming.

The reporter said to her, "You already know that your cousin acted heroically when he saved you and your brother. But now it turns out that Orin's backfire probably saved his family's barn."

"Meg," said her father, taking over from the reporter, "haven't you heard about backfires?"

Meg gulped. "I guess so. I don't really know what they are."

"A backfire is one method of turning away a fire that's coming at you. It's risky, but sometimes it works."

"Risky!" Gran snorted. "It's downright dangerous. It takes skill and courage and . . . more."

Meg looked from the reporter to her parents and then at Gran. Gran's back, Meg thought, as if Gran had been traveling in a distant land and had just returned to her family. Not lost after all.

"Saved the barn," Meg said, trying to let it sink in. "And all the hay," she added. Only now did it occur to her that Orin had tried to explain the backfire to her. "Still," she insisted, "he's sorry." The reporter could talk about heroes all he liked, but that wasn't how Orin regarded what he had done. "Does Uncle Frank have to know about it?" she asked.

"You bet he does," Dad told her. "Frank and Helen will be proud."

"They should be, anyway," Meg said. "Because he took care of us and the horses the best he could."

"Of course," Mom said. "They've already shown Orin how proud they are. We know that."

"And probably they'll be even more proud when they hear about their son's quick thinking and courage. . . ." The reporter was writing these very words on his pad as he spoke them. Then he scratched something out and said, "Ingenuity is what it was. Courage and ingenuity. That's what we'll call it."

34 ". . . and we applaud his courage and ingenuity," concluded the chairman of the Board of Selectmen, reading from a card as he declared Orin Young Hero of the Fire.

But the young hero did not come forward in that crowded, stifling gym.

"Where is he?" whispered Mrs. Boudreau.

"Where is he?" the other grown-ups asked one another.

"Where is he?" demanded a selectman, mounting the makeshift platform to join the other town fathers as they peered out over the crowd.

The kids all nodded. Wasn't it just like Orin, who was short on brainpower, to miss his only moment of glory?

"Out in left field," murmured one of his former classmates. "Where else?"

Meg heard some of these comments as she slipped around the edge of the gym, where everyone had gathered for speeches, presentations, and awards. Out into the parking lot, where a floodlight captured snowflakes in its ample beam.

"Orin!" she shouted. "Orin, wait up!"

Leaving the school grounds, she plunged into white darkness. The cold felt good. This was by no means the first snow, but it seemed magical because there was no wind yet and the buoyant flakes floated awhile before they landed.

She might have looked for Orin's footprints, but she was so sure of where he had gone that she just ran straight out to the road.

She had to cross the bridge before heading for the town green. In the dark, with snow filling the deep spaces of the

130

night, it almost seemed as if Prescott Falls were whole again. Of course rebuilding was under way. But that wasn't what gave her the impression of the town as it had been before the fire. The sense of the place came from within her. It was so vivid in her mind's eye that she felt as if she were running backward through time. She could almost believe that if she ran hard enough, she would arrive in her own past.

Two lights guided her across the road, one over the gas pump in front of Libby's Market, the other in front of the boxlike prefab building that was the temporary fire and police station.

At the edge of the green she faltered. She had been sure Orin would come to the war memorial. She had imagined him standing up to it, his bulky figure taller than the slanted stone. But there was no sign of him there.

Baffled, she started to turn away. That was when she saw the dark lump huddled at the base of the war memorial. Orin? She walked toward it, scuffing the fresh snow so that he would hear her coming and not be startled.

But he never moved.

His stillness was unnerving. What if she found him crying? She had never seen him cry, not even when Toby had to be shot. What would she say to him?

Drawing closer, she saw that he was squatting, with one hand extended, touching the memorial. Dropping down beside him, she let out a little gasp as her bare knees sank into the snow. She did not speak. She just waited with him.

Finally he withdrew his hand from the name on the stone. Without turning to her, he said, "I'm not Champ."

"Of course you're not," she agreed.

"That's what they want."

"Yes," she answered. "I guess they do. Want Champ. So do you. But he's dead, Orin. They have you, though. Only

131

they didn't know it exactly. Not before." She paused. She wasn't getting this right. "Maybe they didn't know, but now they do. Sort of."

Orin shook his head. "I'm not Champ."

She grabbed his arm. "No one expects you to be like Champ." She needed to get him away from thinking about his brother. "Listen, Orin," she said, "there can be different kinds of heroes." But she needed to play down the hero talk, too. "You've been called a whole lot of awful things, haven't you? So what do you care if some people call you a hero? It's a lot closer to the truth than those other names."

Orin looked at her without speaking. Then he stood, pulling her up with him. "Here's the hero," he said, leaning forward and brushing his fingers across his brother's name.

She knew he wasn't about to give in. Then an idea came to her. "You know what Gran's been like," she told him. "But I bet you don't know that since we moved into the lodge, she's been pining for you. She could tell that you were churning over something, but she couldn't figure out what it was. Then when that reporter got this whole thing going about you and the backfire, everything started to make sense for her. Only now she feels terrible because she thinks she gave up on you when you needed her. She says she doubts she can put things right again, because she's too old. She told Mom she needs her own walls around her and her own grandson to fuss over. Do you hear me, Orin? How do you think she'll feel if you don't go in there and get your award?"

Meg waited a moment. Was Orin thinking this over? What could he make of all that she was saying?

"Gran's talking?" he finally asked.

"Some," she answered truthfully. "At times she still goes quiet. Maybe with you helping out she'll get even better. You know how you blame yourself for Toby getting burned?"

She could see Orin's slow nod.

"Well, Gran blames herself the same way. Blames herself for losing track of you. She shouldn't, but that's the way she is. You running away from the gym, that's just getting yourself lost all over again. Proving her right."

"No," Orin almost shouted. "I'm not lost."

"Gran will think you are if you don't come back. She's always been for you, Orin, just like Champ. Now you have to help her."

"Help Gran? Me?"

"You," Meg confirmed. "You, Orin. No one else." Feeling him pull away from the memorial, she spoke again. "Come on. Let's get back while there's time."

They left the green and stomped through the snow to the bridge. On the far side Orin seemed to lose heart. Meg made a point of pushing forward, almost running, even though the snow was beginning to pile up now and made for slippery footing.

Inside the school Orin stopped, panic written on his tight shoulders and clenched hands.

"It's all right," she told him. "Gran's in there, wondering. Worrying."

He followed her down the hall to the gym.

35 Uncle Frank came striding toward them, snow melting on his hair, his jacket. Meg saw him arrange his expression to register unconcern. She guessed he was afraid of scaring Orin off.

"You're all right, then," he remarked to Orin. Not quite a question. "I'd better tell them." Then he added, keeping his tone mild, "They were a mite fussed, your ma and Gran."

Meg wondered whether Orin understood that his dad had

133

been worried, too. More than somewhat, as Gran would say. Did Orin even realize that Uncle Frank had been outside looking for him? There was no way of telling, because already Orin had sealed himself off. Maybe the only way he could deal with praise was the way he protected himself against taunts. Seeing him like this, his shoulders slightly hunched, his eyes empty of expression, she knew that he was preparing to endure what was to come.

But she wished that she had mentioned Uncle Frank. Out there on the snowy green she should have reminded Orin that his father had called him old son long before there had been any hero talk. That day after the fire, after Toby was shot. She couldn't reach Orin now. She could only keep him moving in the right direction.

Ahead of him, turning at the door to the gym, Uncle Frank paused and said, "We'll be up front together. The selectmen asked for one of us to be there with you." Then he forged ahead through the crowd.

As Meg shoved Orin through the door, Joan Barter was making her way to the portable platform. Everyone clapped. Lined up at the front on either side were kids with dogs and cats and rabbits and one goat. And Paul hugging his house flowers.

Meg couldn't figure out what Joan had to do with all this until she heard someone pounding out chords on a piano. Were they going to let that girl sing? She must have complained a lot about being left out of all the fun, so that finally they were forced to give her something to do.

Joan clasped her hands and raised her face to the audience, her Judy Garland pose. " 'Somewhere over the rainbow,' " Joan started to sing. But the words weren't straight out of *The Wizard of Oz*. Someone had slipped in phrases about looking beyond the fire to a new horizon where not only bluebirds sing, but also those who suffered losses last October. Some relation of Joan's must have made up this version. Why else would they let this kid with a voice like a screech owl perform before the entire town and a bunch of well-heeled outsiders?

Joan hit a high note, held on to it, flung her arms wide, and scooped to the next note above it. But not alone. One of the house flowers let loose with a spirited response, no mere cluck, but a series of squawks that rose to a trill and all but drowned out Joan's voice.

Joan swung around until she located the vocalizing hen. She fixed its holder with a look of fury. Paul, fumbling to grasp the offending beak, lost his grip on the other hen, which flew up to the basketball hoop. From that lofty perch she, too, burst into song. Hers was the high, sustained note of a true soprano. For a moment it seemed more in tune with the piano than the human singer, who persisted valiantly to the bitter end of her song.

By now the gym rocked with mirth, although everyone politely applauded when Joan took her bow.

It wasn't until all the children, each with a special prize or ribbon, had led or carried their pets back to the section of the gym reserved for them that Joan managed to scramble ahead and block Paul's way.

Meg couldn't stand by and let her bully him in front of all these people. Pushing Orin toward the front, where the presenters were trying to restore some dignity to the occasion, she cut through the rows.

She was nearly there now. She could hear Joan blasting Paul as she loomed over him. But before Meg could reach them, the chairman of the Board of Selectmen snatched Paul away. Carrying Paul to the platform, the selectman lifted him up to the basketball hoop to retrieve the hen, which continued to hold forth until Paul stuck her inside his sweater with the other one.

Everyone clapped and cheered. Meg had no idea whether

people were applauding the selectman or Paul or the hen. She couldn't get her mind off Joan. And then, even as Meg cringed with embarrassment for Paul, she saw him march toward her. Proudly he clutched the bulges inside his sweater. He was beaming.

"Guess what?" he whispered. "Joan thinks I did it on purpose. She thinks I trained Grace and Disgrace to sing with her. Louder than her."

"Never mind," Meg said, fed up with bullies. She knew what Gran would say, but how could a small shy kid like Paul ever get anywhere with someone who was meaner and bigger and always took advantage of him? "I'll set Joan straight," Meg told him grimly.

"No!" Paul's whisper came out a muted shout.

"Look at her, Paul. She's talking to all the kids. She needs to be taken down—"

"No!"

"She's spreading lies about you."

"I know," he declared, grinning broadly. "I'll be the only one in my school with trick hens." And with what came close to a swagger, he pushed his way into the cluster of children with their survival pets. Careful to hold on to the bottom of his sweater, he took his place among them.

By now quiet was restored to the gym. Someone motioned Meg to the floor just as Orin, prodded a bit by Eddie Kresky, stepped up to the platform. There was Uncle Frank, looking every bit as uncomfortable as his son. He reached out to Orin, who seemed uncertain where to stand. *Here*, beckoned Uncle Frank's hand. *With me.*

The town fathers nodded and beamed. Turning to face them, Orin shuffled backward until he fetched up beside Uncle Frank. There they stood, father and son, as stiff as relatives pictured in Gran's family album. Along with the awkward pose, Meg recognized some of the features she had glimpsed in those cracked and faded portaits. The photographs were gone now, burned, but not the images she held in memory.

Meg imagined Gran nodding at the sight of her son and grandson side by side. Gran must be fixing the two of them in her mind to return to later on when she felt like reminding herself of this important occasion in the lives of them all.

AUTHOR'S NOTE

In October 1947, after a summerlong drought, wildfires in Maine devastated vast areas of woodland and some entire communities. Although fire fighting had not yet developed in organization and technology to its present-day level, volunteers and desperately needed equipment poured into the state to join local efforts to save people and houses and farms and businesses and wildlife and the forests themselves. Many of the places mentioned in this book are real and suffered extensive damage. But Prescott Falls and surrounding towns are fictional, as are the people whose stories are told here.